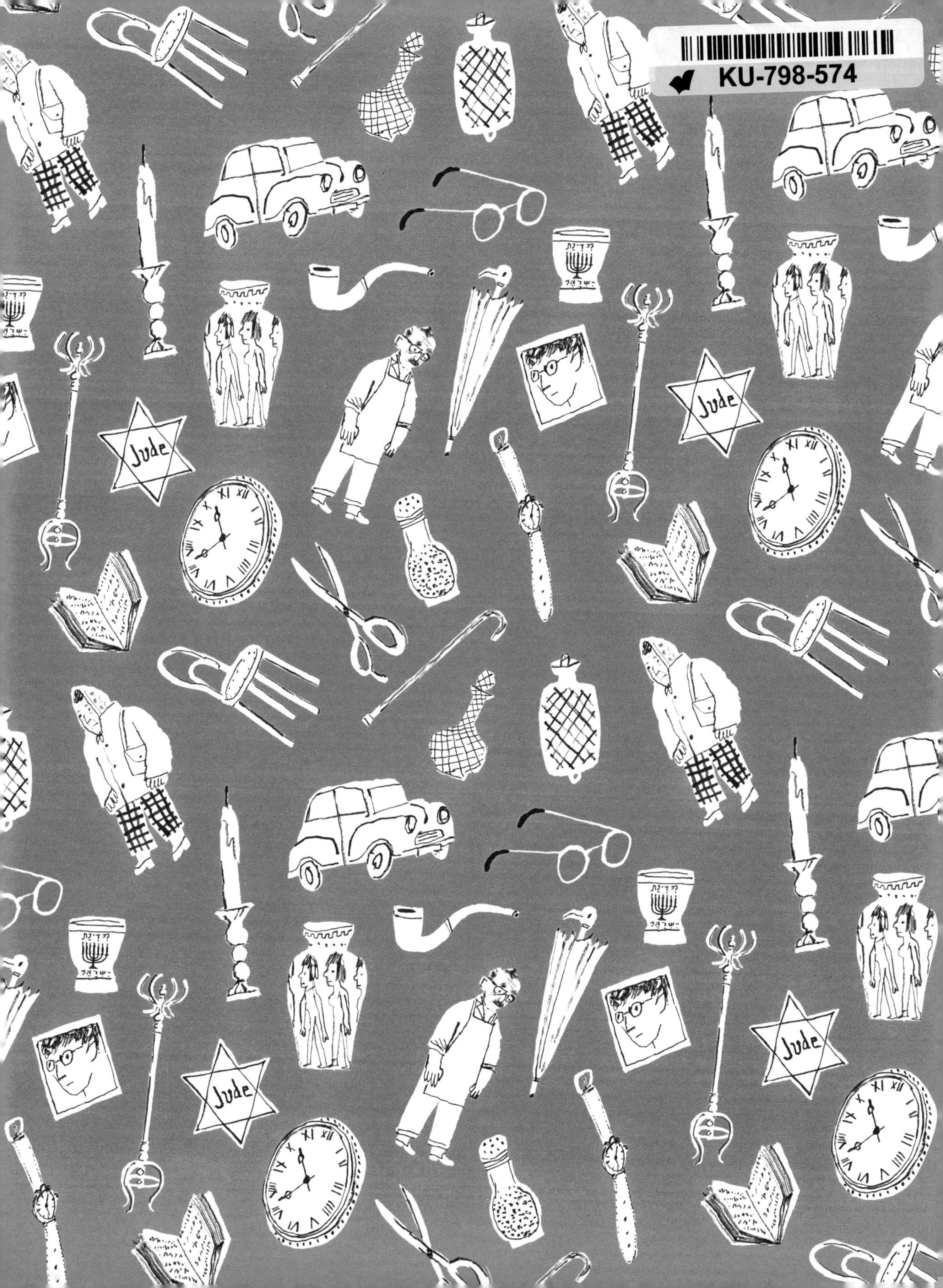
Jude
Jude
Jude
Jude

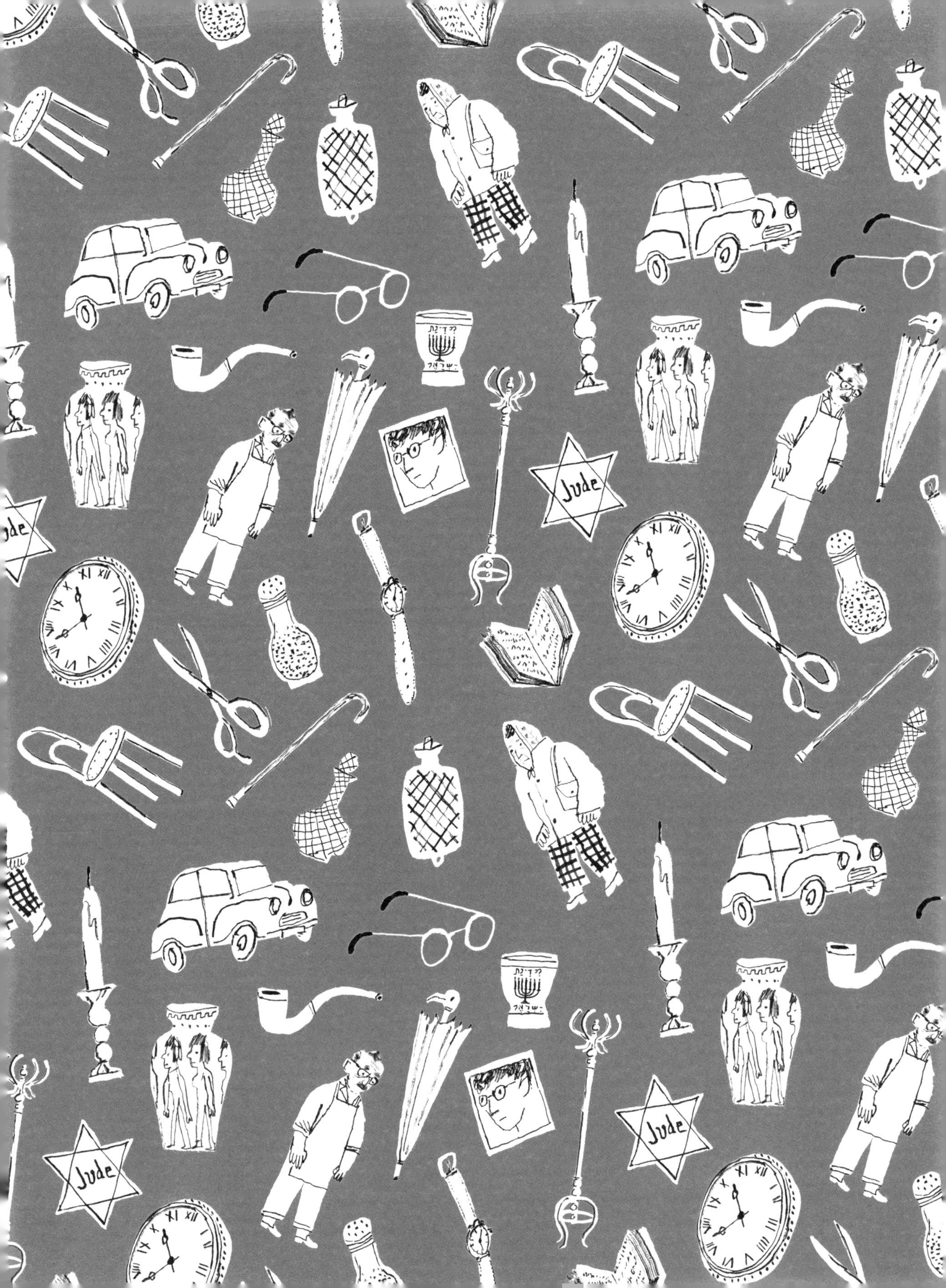
Jude
Jude
Jude
Jude

A PERSON'S HEART IS LIKE A SAUSAGE.
NO ONE KNOWS EXACTLY WHAT'S INSIDE.
— YIDDISH PROVERB.

FOR ALL THE BUBBES INCLUDING
ESTHER, JOAN, NOMMI & VIOLETTE.
— B.P & Z.H

ALTE ZACHEN*

ZIGGY HANAOR / BENJAMIN PHILLIPS

* OLD THINGS

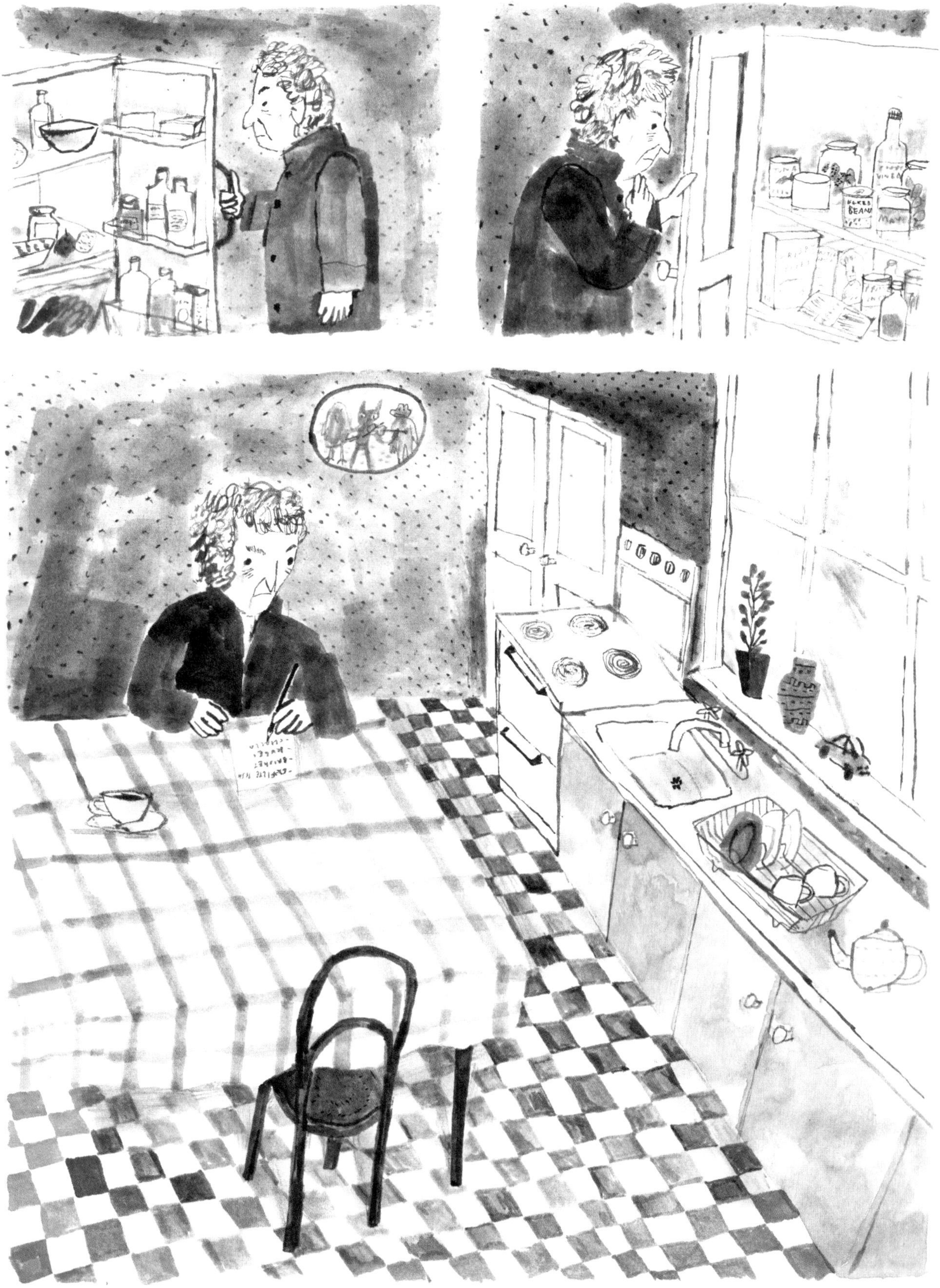
TUNA

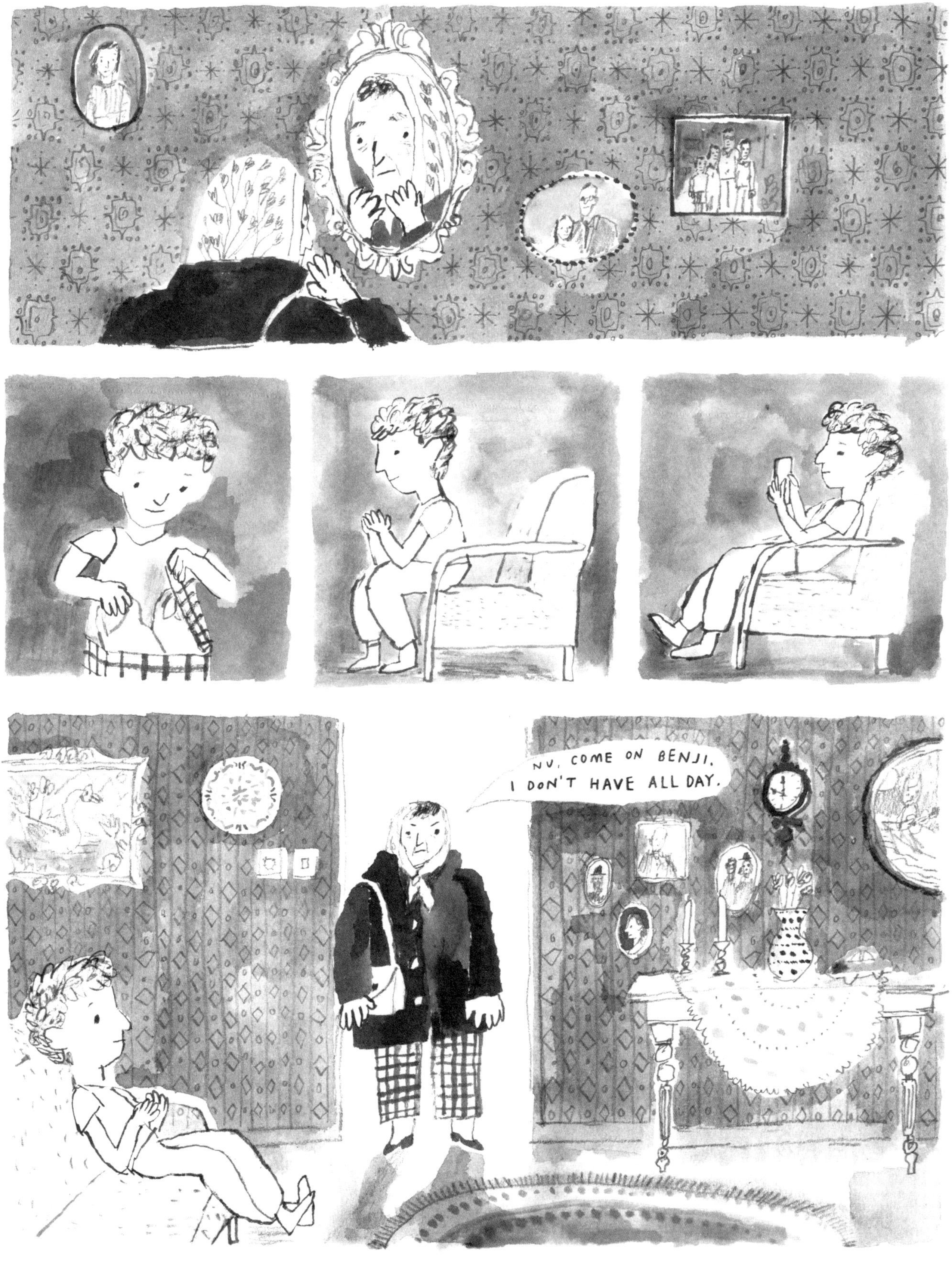
NU, COME ON BENJI. I DON'T HAVE ALL DAY.

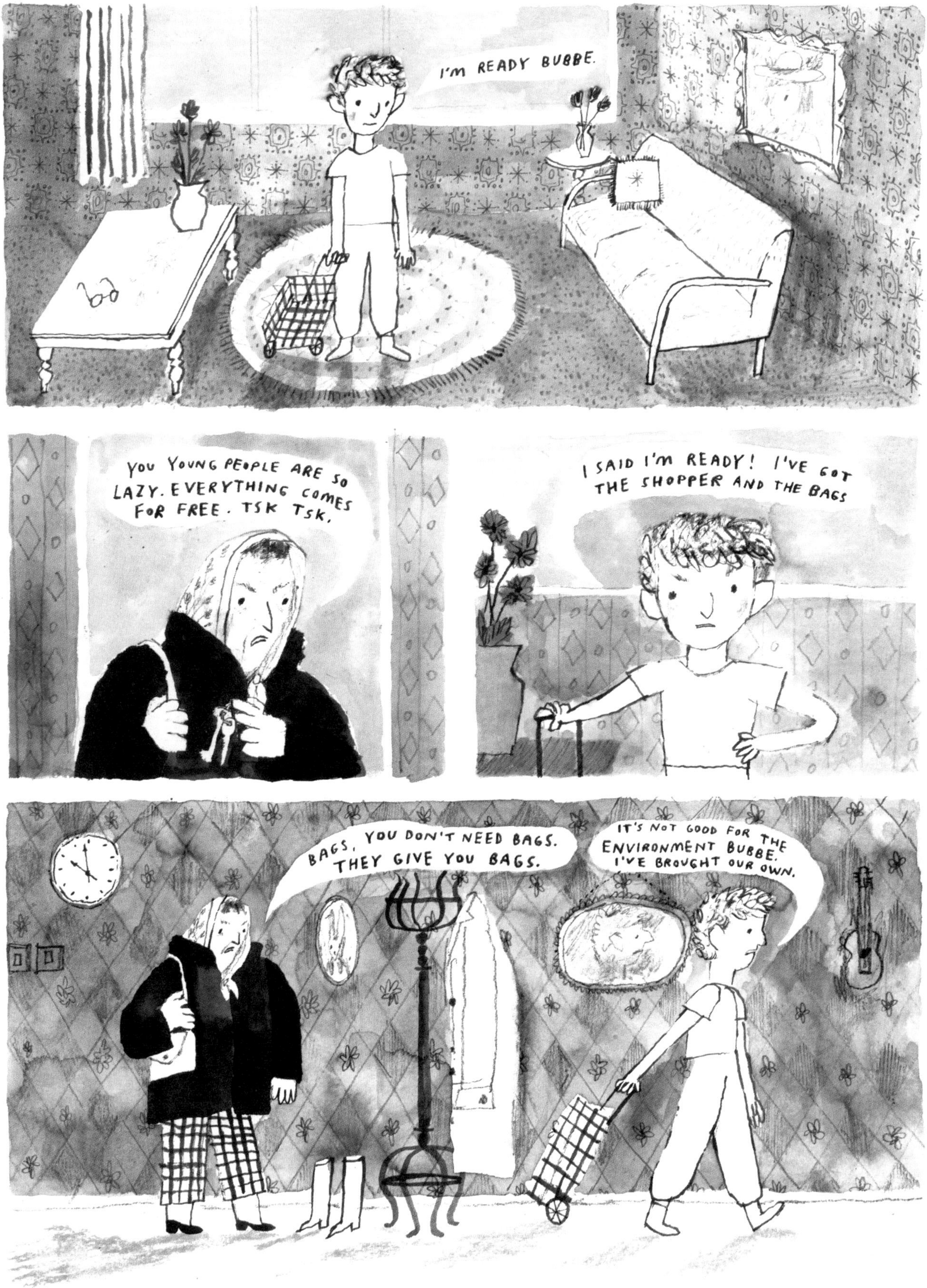
I'M READY BUBBE.
YOU YOUNG PEOPLE ARE SO LAZY. EVERYTHING COMES FOR FREE. TSK TSK.
I SAID I'M READY! I'VE GOT THE SHOPPER AND THE BAGS
BAGS, YOU DON'T NEED BAGS. THEY GIVE YOU BAGS.
IT'S NOT GOOD FOR THE ENVIRONMENT BUBBE. I'VE BROUGHT OUR OWN.

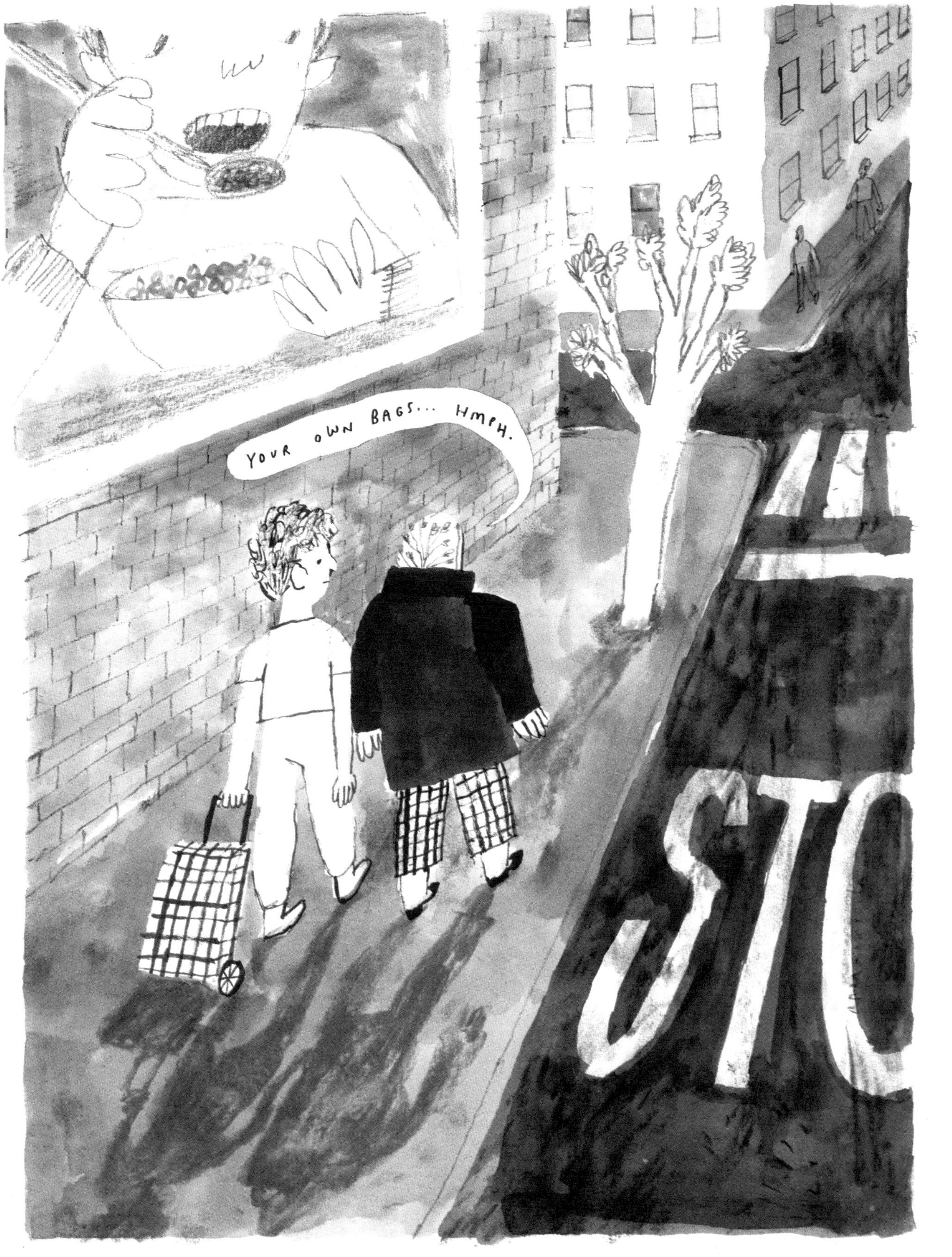
YOUR OWN BAGS... HMPH.

WHAT TO EAT THIS EVENING? AH, WE'LL HAVE GEFILTE FISH.

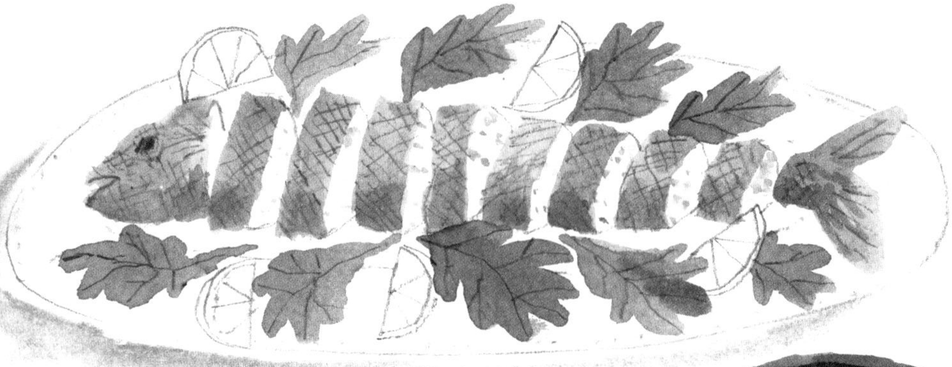

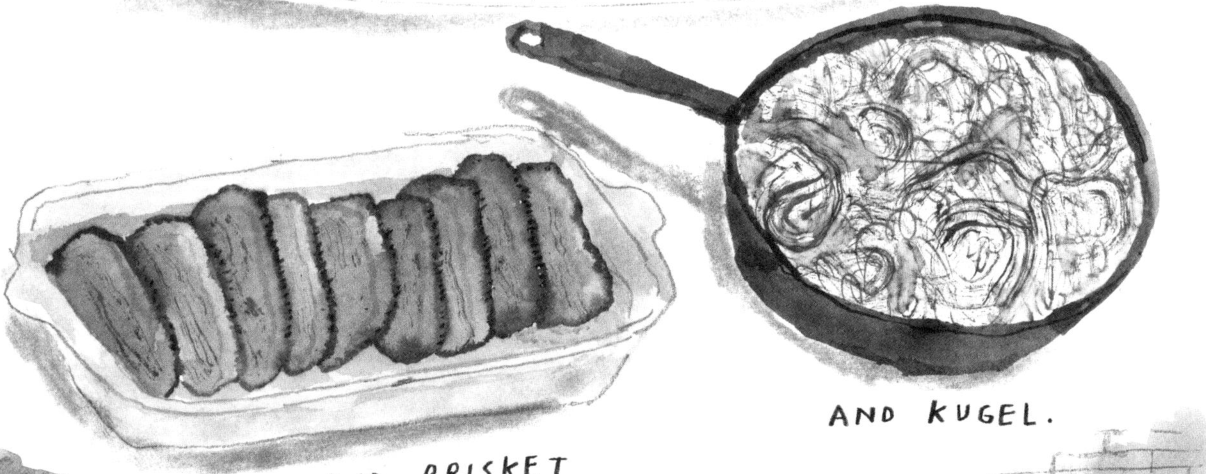

AND KUGEL.

AND BRISKET

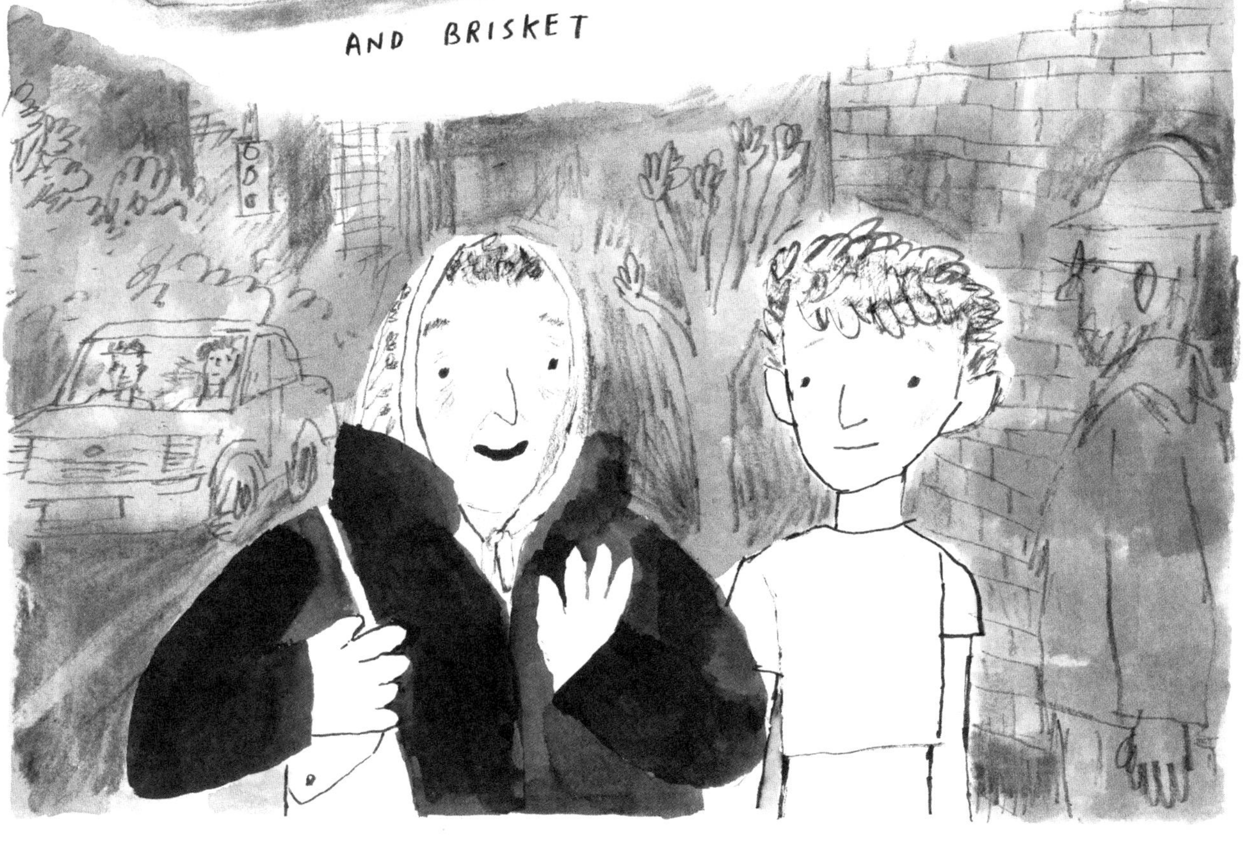

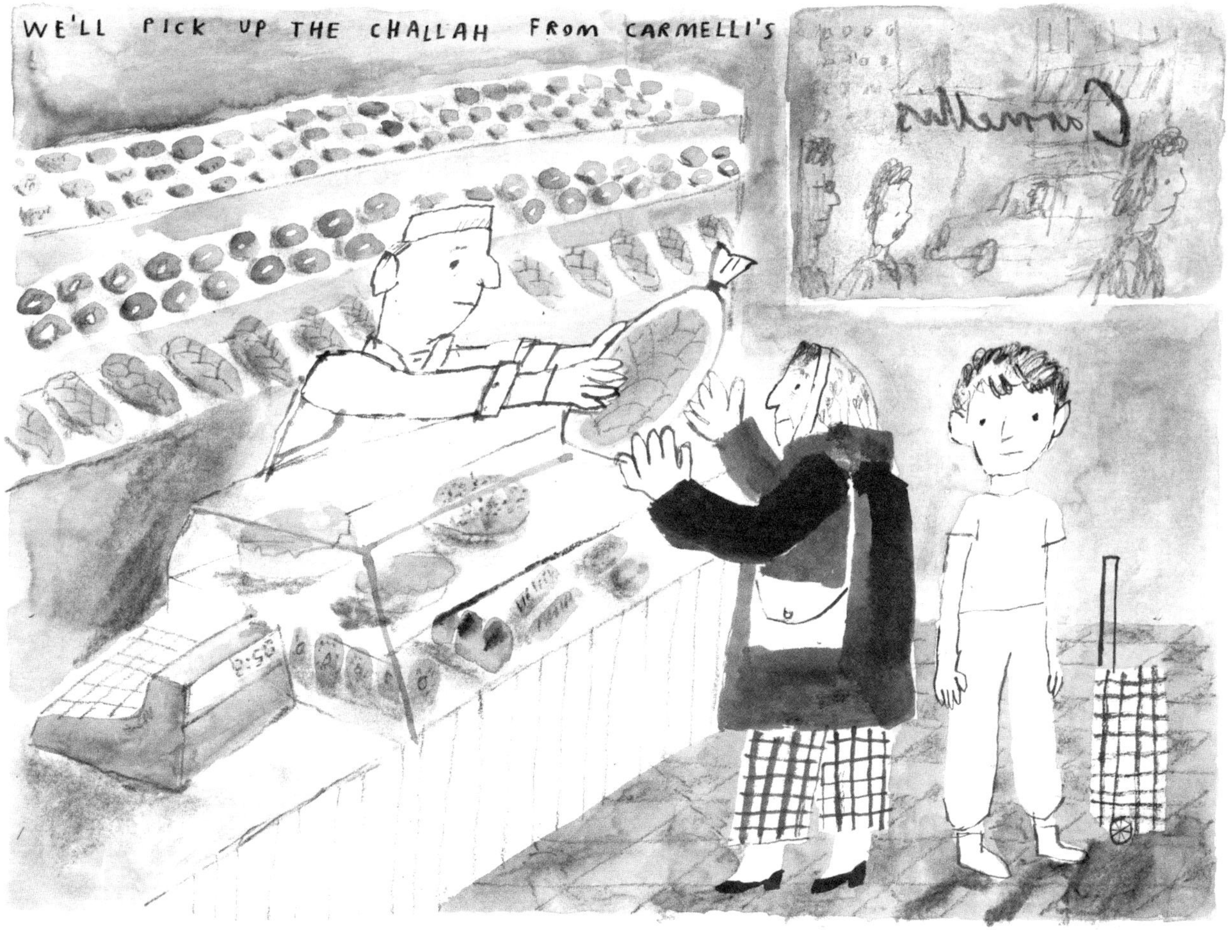
WE'LL PICK UP THE CHALLAH FROM CARMELLI'S

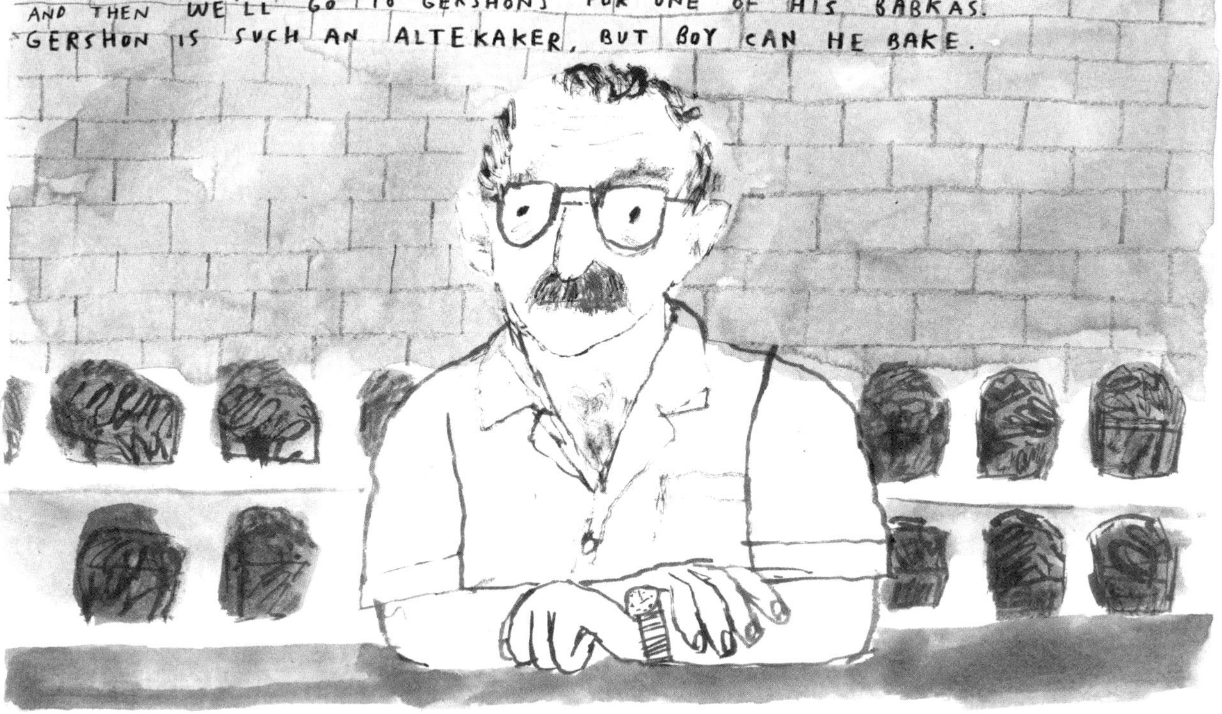
AND THEN WE'LL GO TO GERSHON'S FOR ONE OF HIS BABKAS.
GERSHON IS SUCH AN ALTEKAKER, BUT BOY CAN HE BAKE.

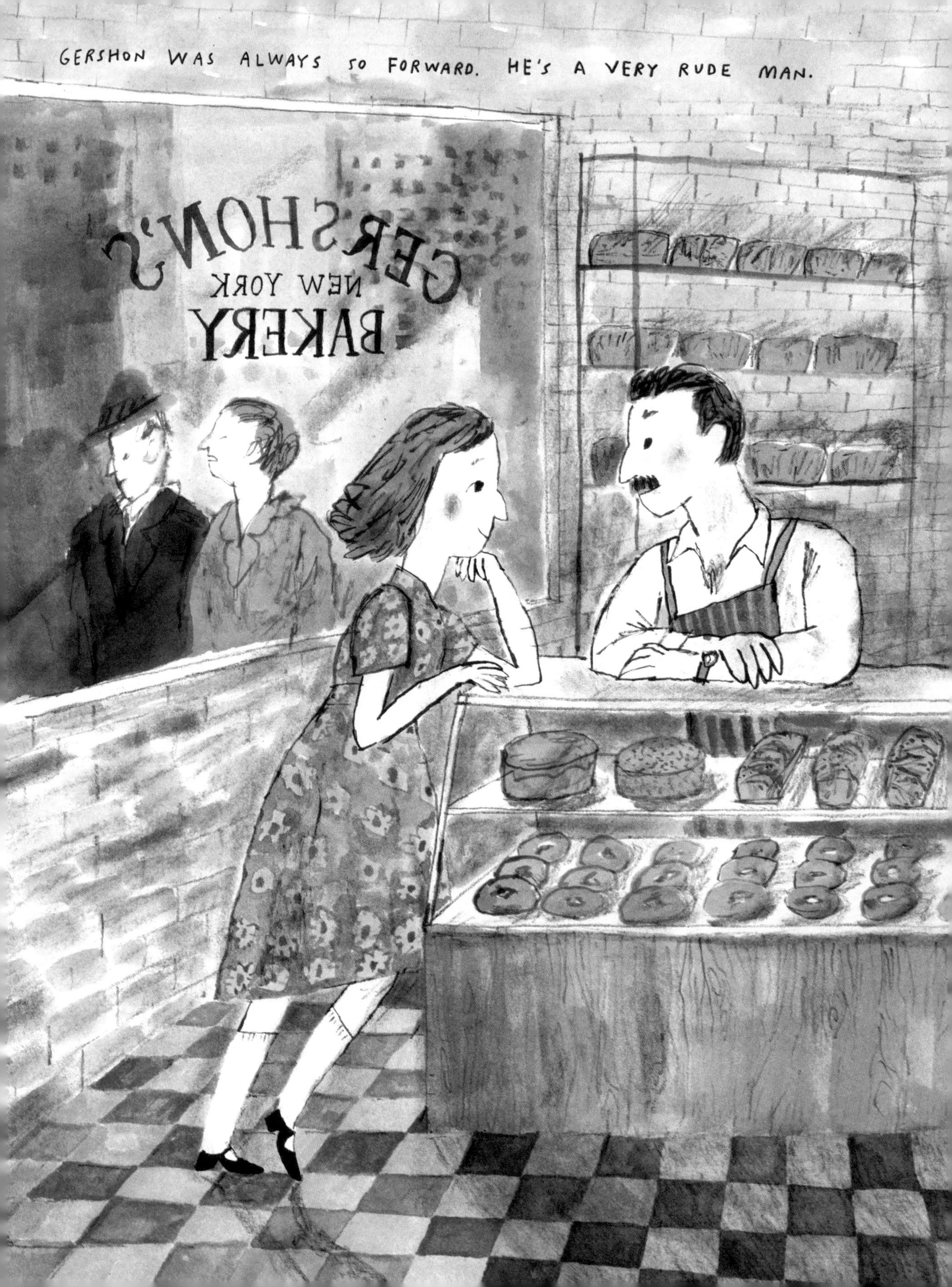
GERSHON WAS ALWAYS SO FORWARD. HE'S A VERY RUDE MAN.
GERSHON'S NEW YORK BAKERY

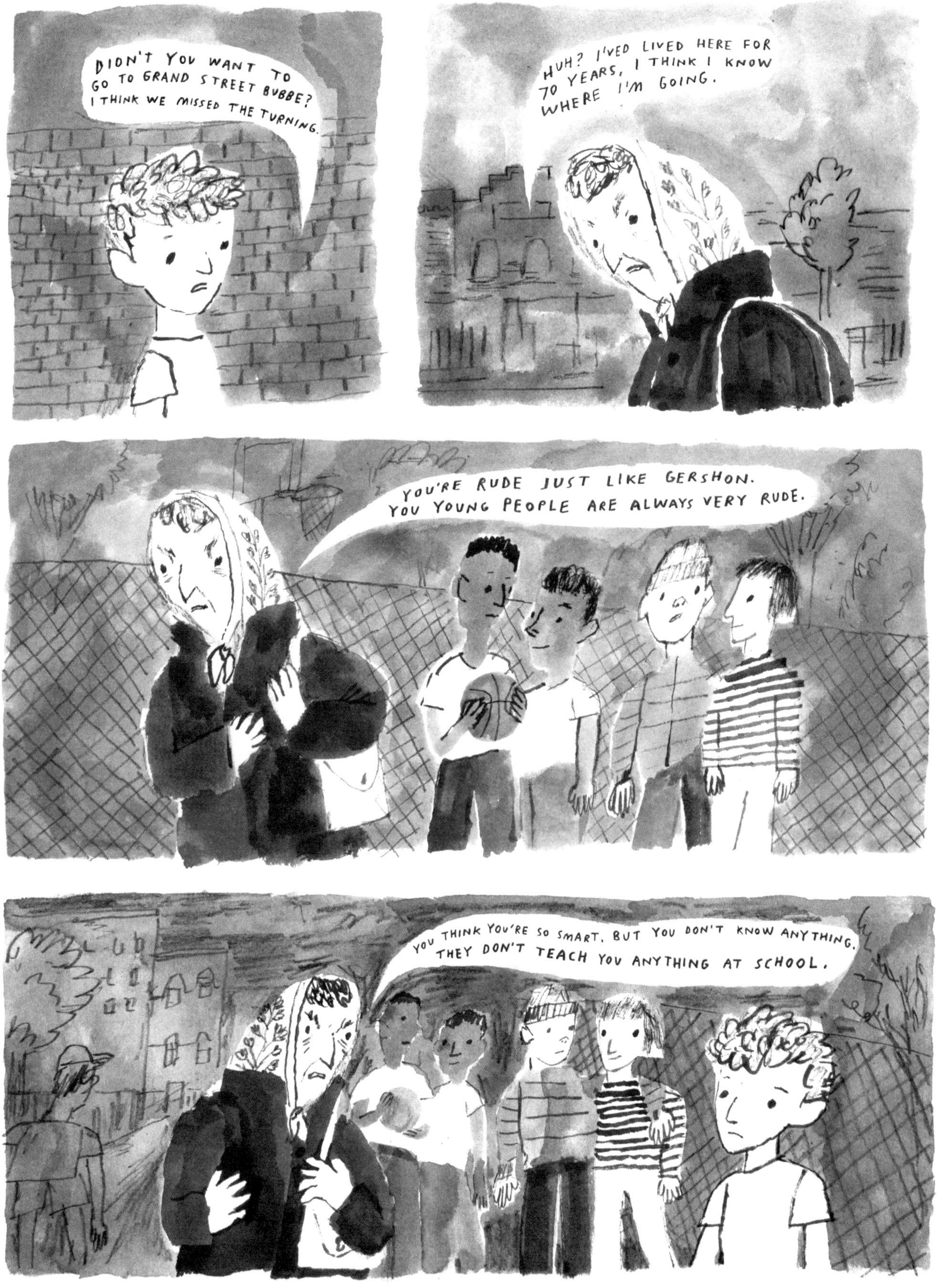
DIDN'T YOU WANT TO GO TO GRAND STREET BUBBE? I THINK WE MISSED THE TURNING.
HUH? I'VED LIVED HERE FOR 70 YEARS, I THINK I KNOW WHERE I'M GOING.
YOU'RE RUDE JUST LIKE GERSHON. YOU YOUNG PEOPLE ARE ALWAYS VERY RUDE.
YOU THINK YOU'RE SO SMART, BUT YOU DON'T KNOW ANYTHING. THEY DON'T TEACH YOU ANYTHING AT SCHOOL.

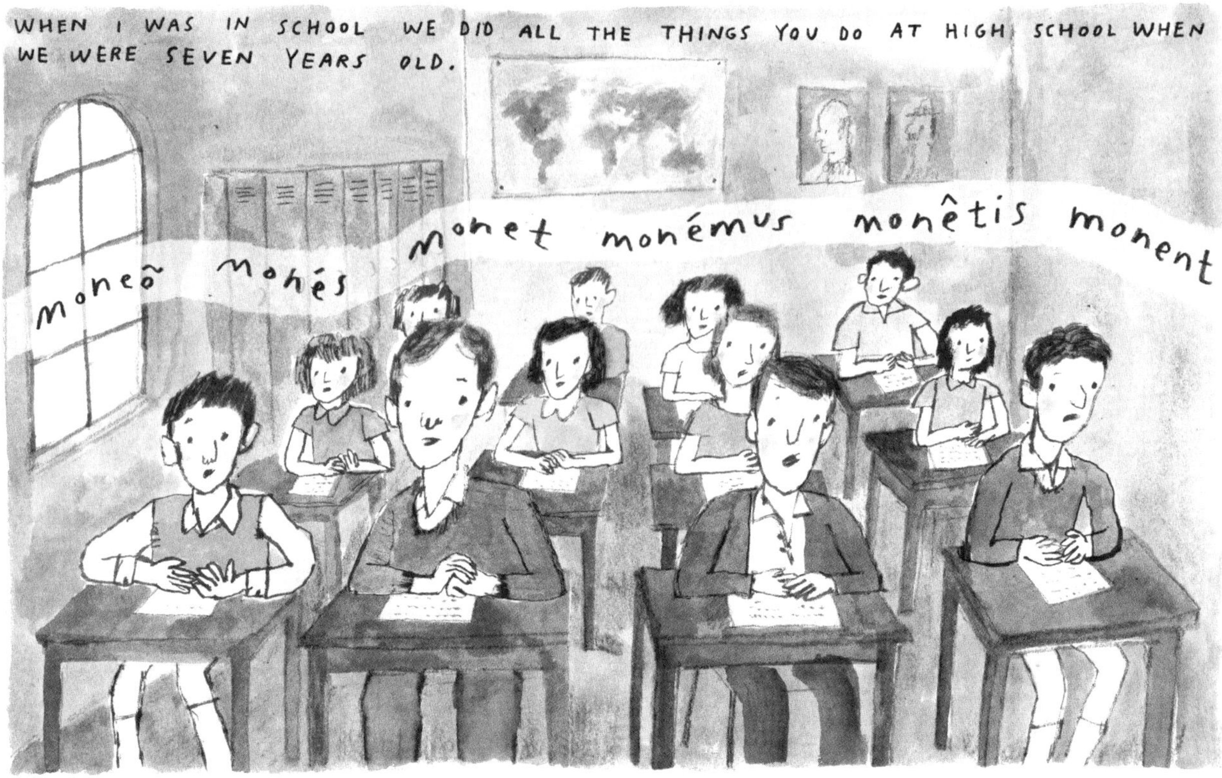
WHEN I WAS IN SCHOOL WE DID ALL THE THINGS YOU DO AT HIGH SCHOOL WHEN WE WERE SEVEN YEARS OLD.
moneõ monés monet monémus monêtis monent

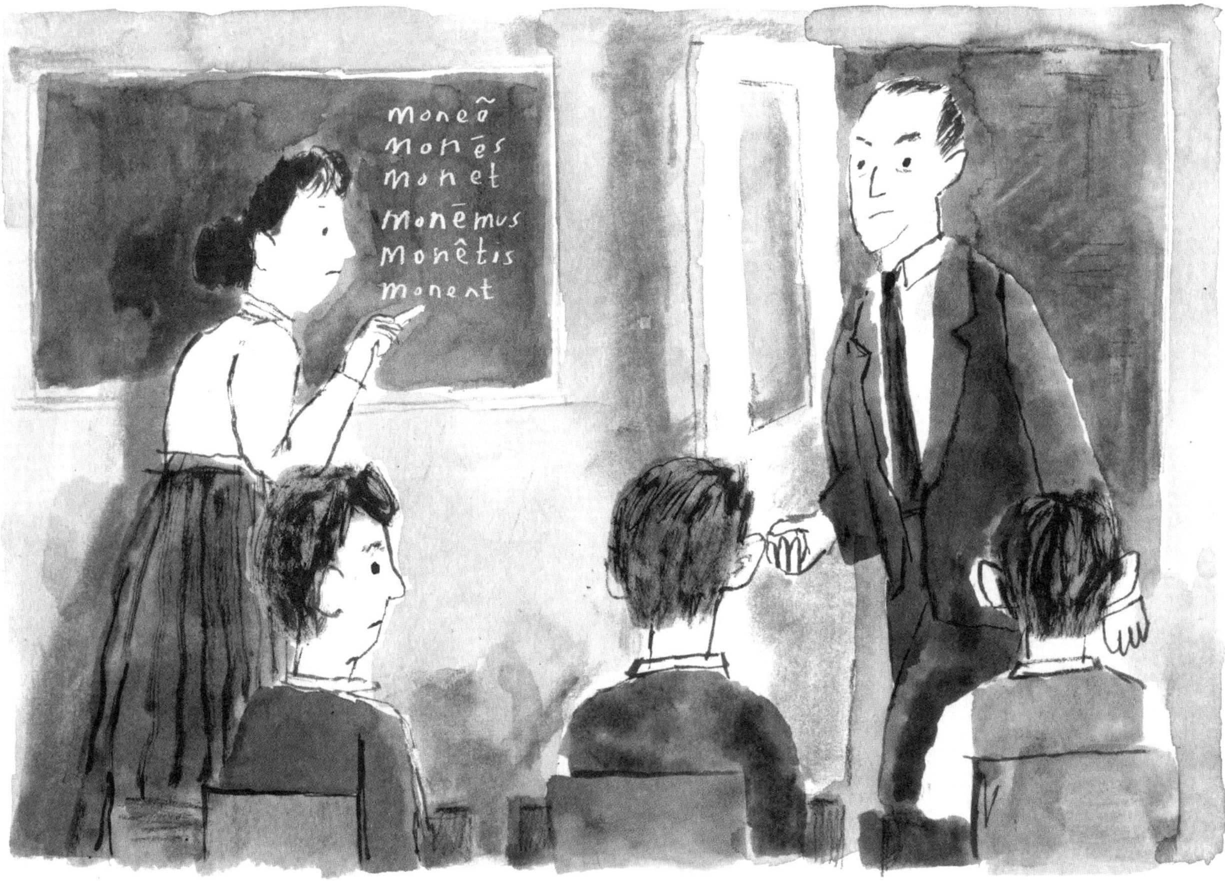
moneõ
monés
monet
monēmus
monêtis
monent

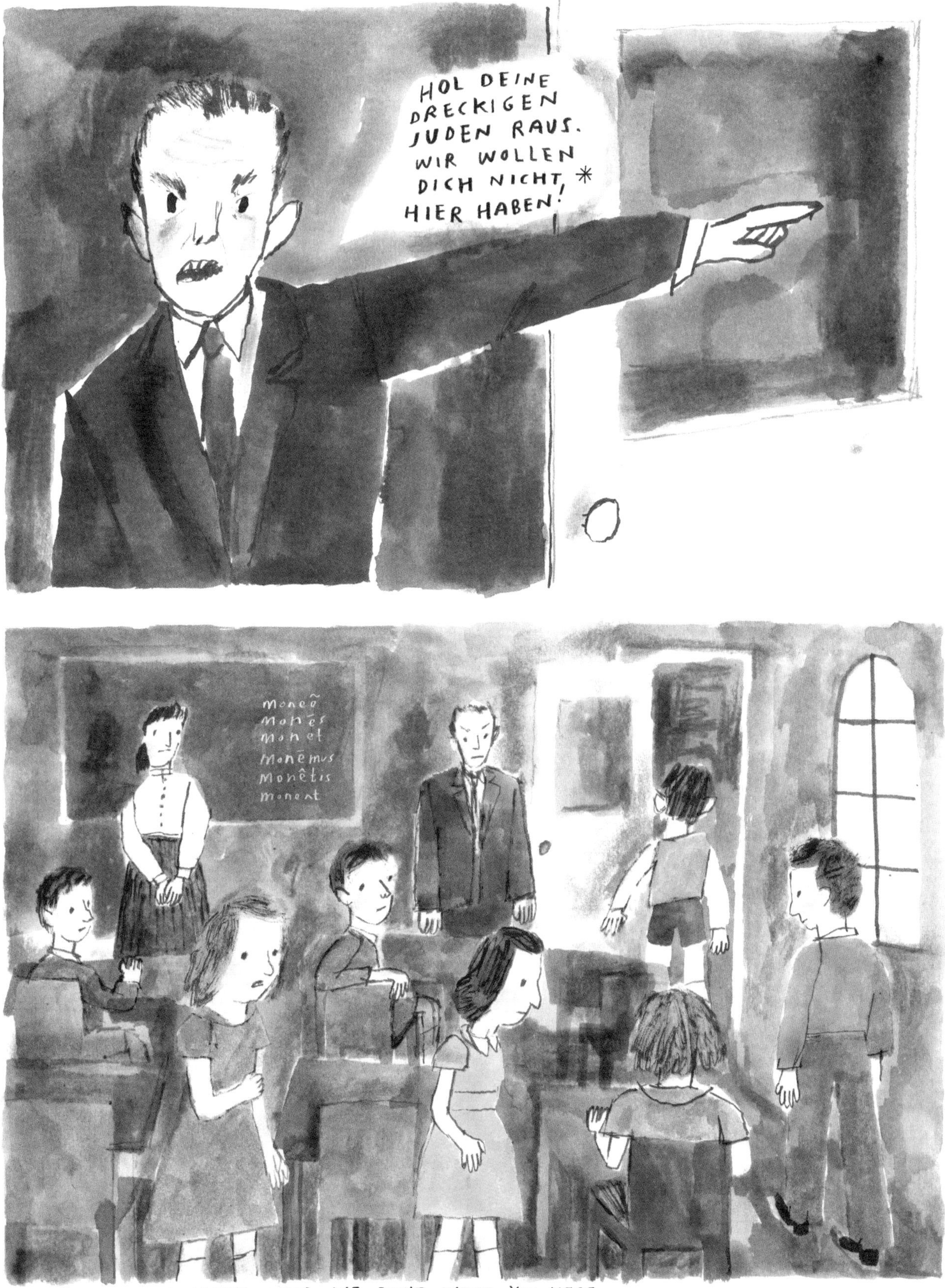
HOL DEINE DRECKIGEN JUDEN RAUS. WIR WOLLEN DICH NICHT, HIER HABEN! *
moneõ
monēs
monet
monēmus
monêtis
monent

* GET OUT YOU DIRTY JEWS. WE DON'T WANT YOU HERE.

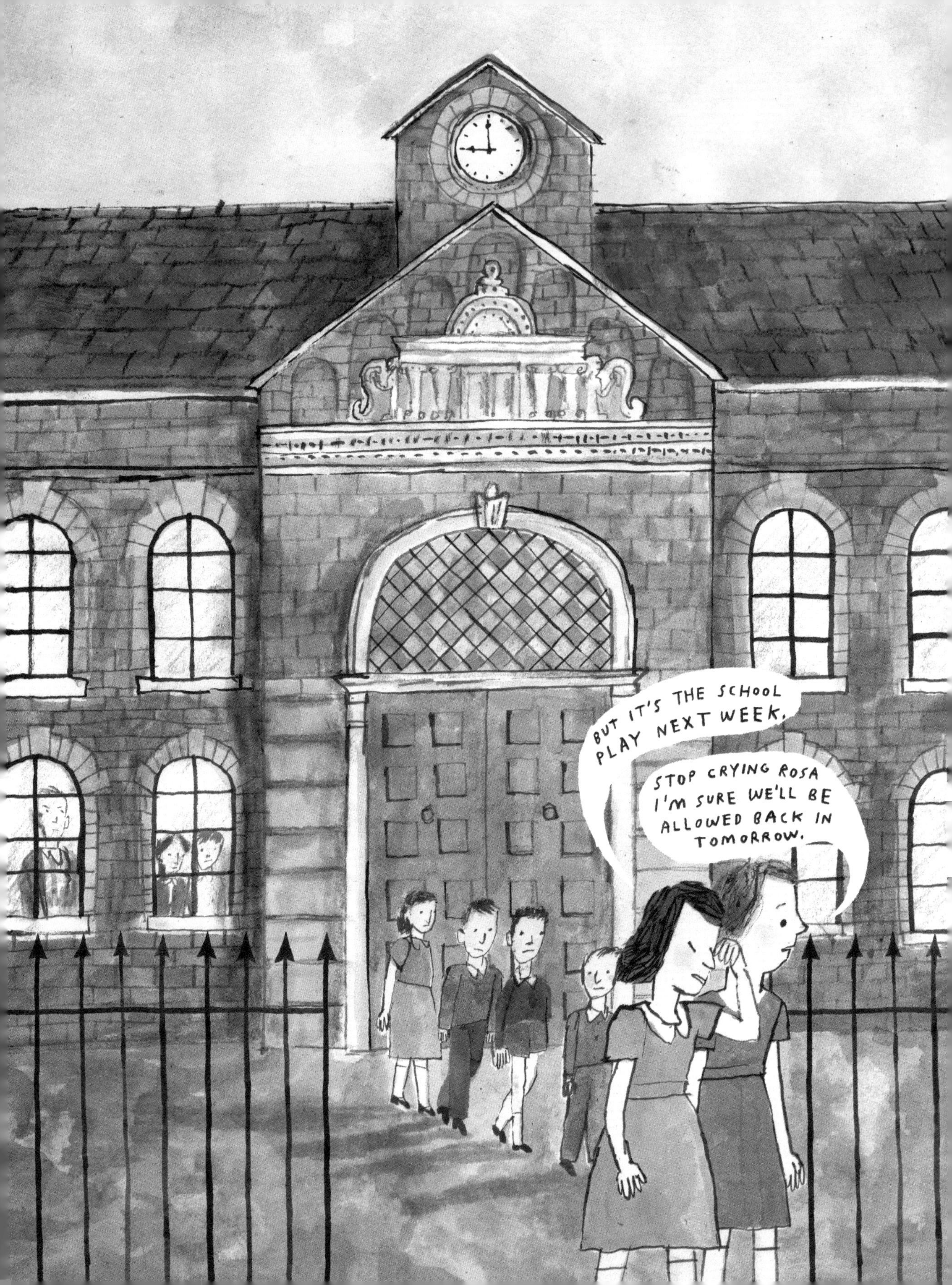
BUT IT'S THE SCHOOL PLAY NEXT WEEK.
STOP CRYING ROSA I'M SURE WE'LL BE ALLOWED BACK IN TOMORROW.

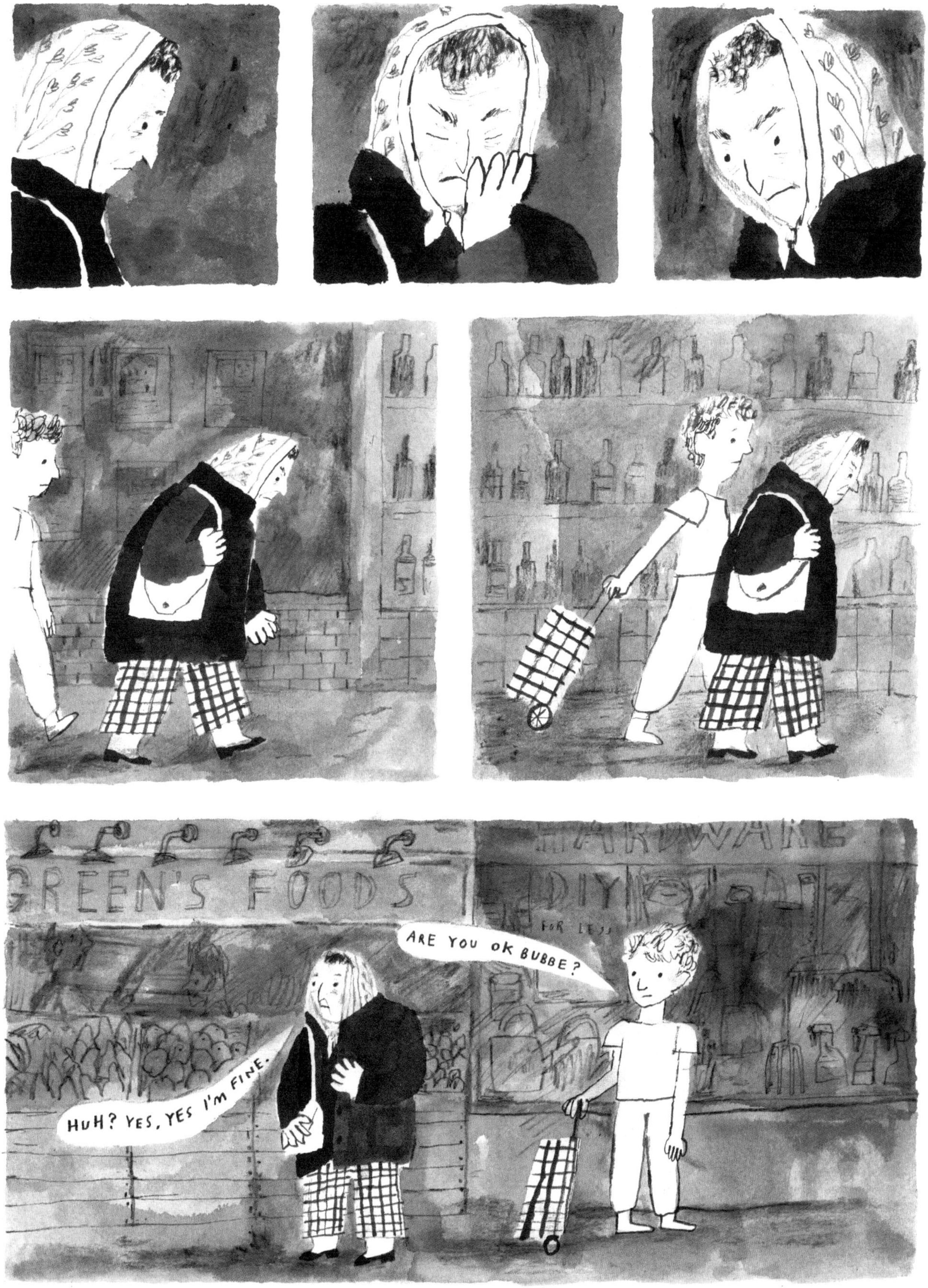
GREEN'S FOODS
DIY
ARE YOU OK BUBBE?
HUH? YES, YES I'M FINE.

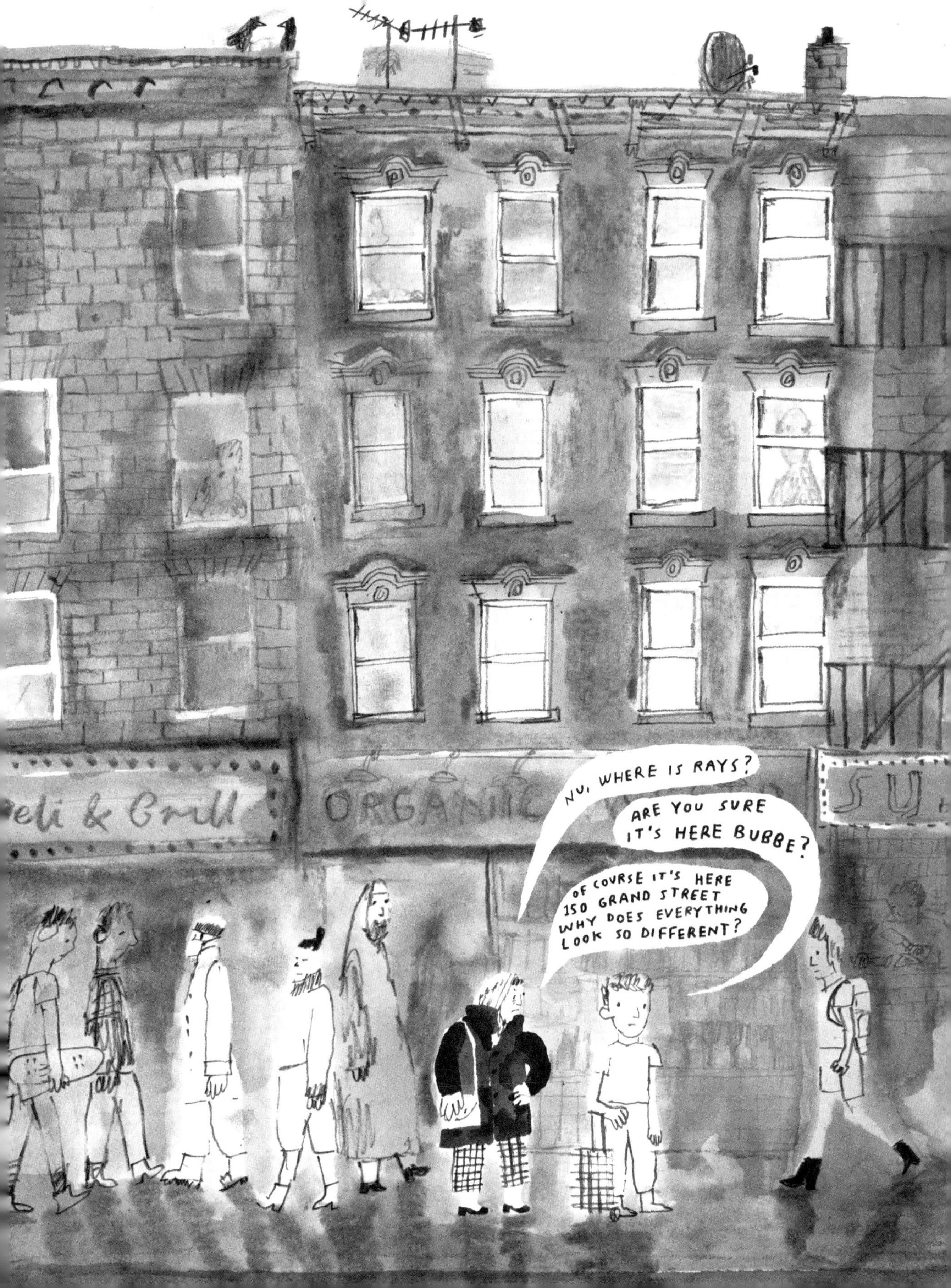
NU, WHERE IS RAYS?
ARE YOU SURE IT'S HERE BUBBE?
OF COURSE IT'S HERE 150 GRAND STREET WHY DOES EVERYTHING LOOK SO DIFFERENT?
eli & Grill
ORGANIC

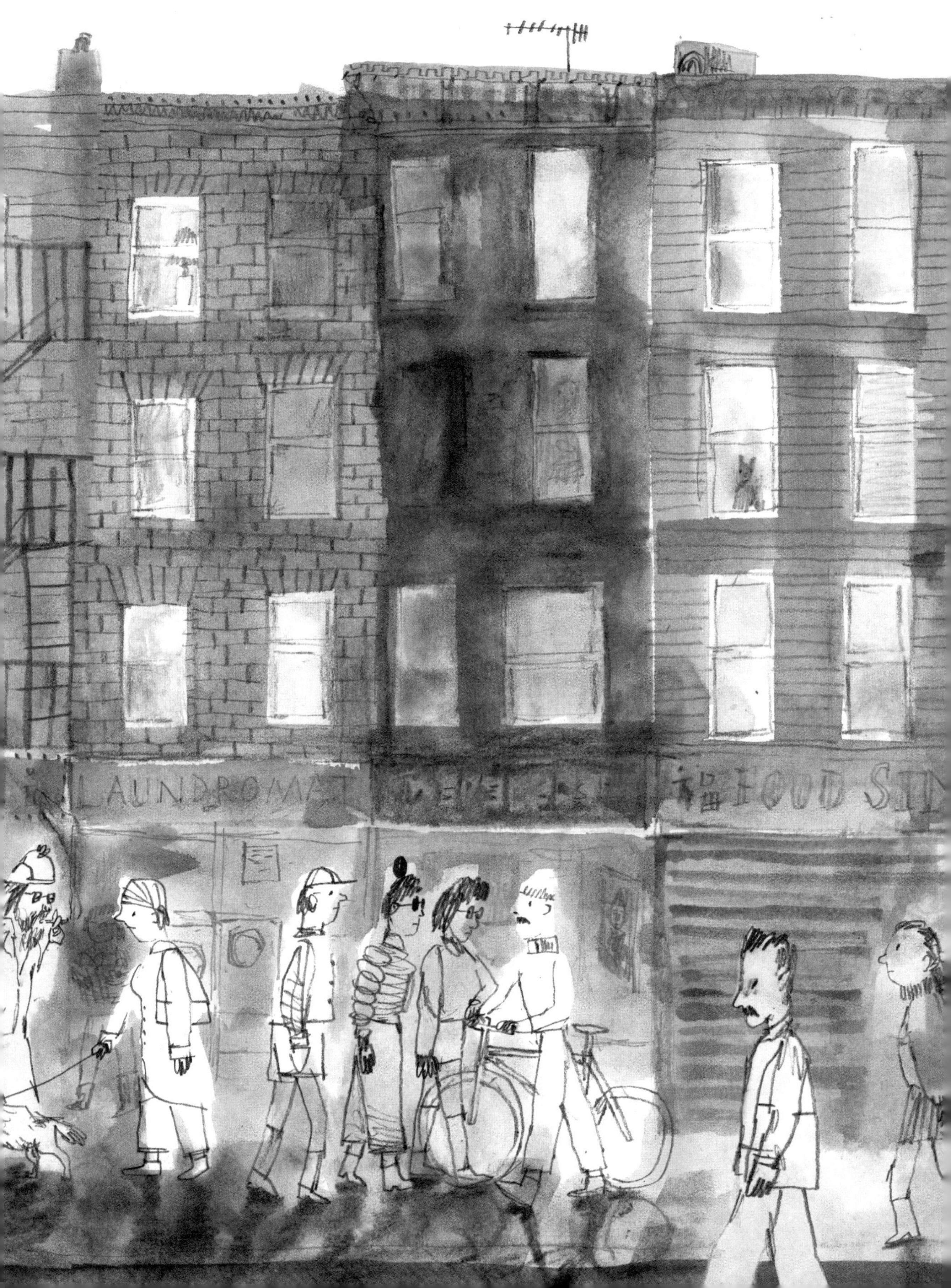
LAUNDROMAT
FOOD

RAY CAME OVER ON THE BOAT WITH YOUR ZAYDE JOE, ZICHRONO LEBRACHA. RAY WOULD NEVER MOVE HIS SHOP. THE ONLY CHANGE HE EVER MADE IN HIS LIFE WAS GETTING ON THAT BOAT WITH YOUR ZAYDE JOE. AND THAT WAS ONLY BECAUSE HE HAD NO CHOICE.

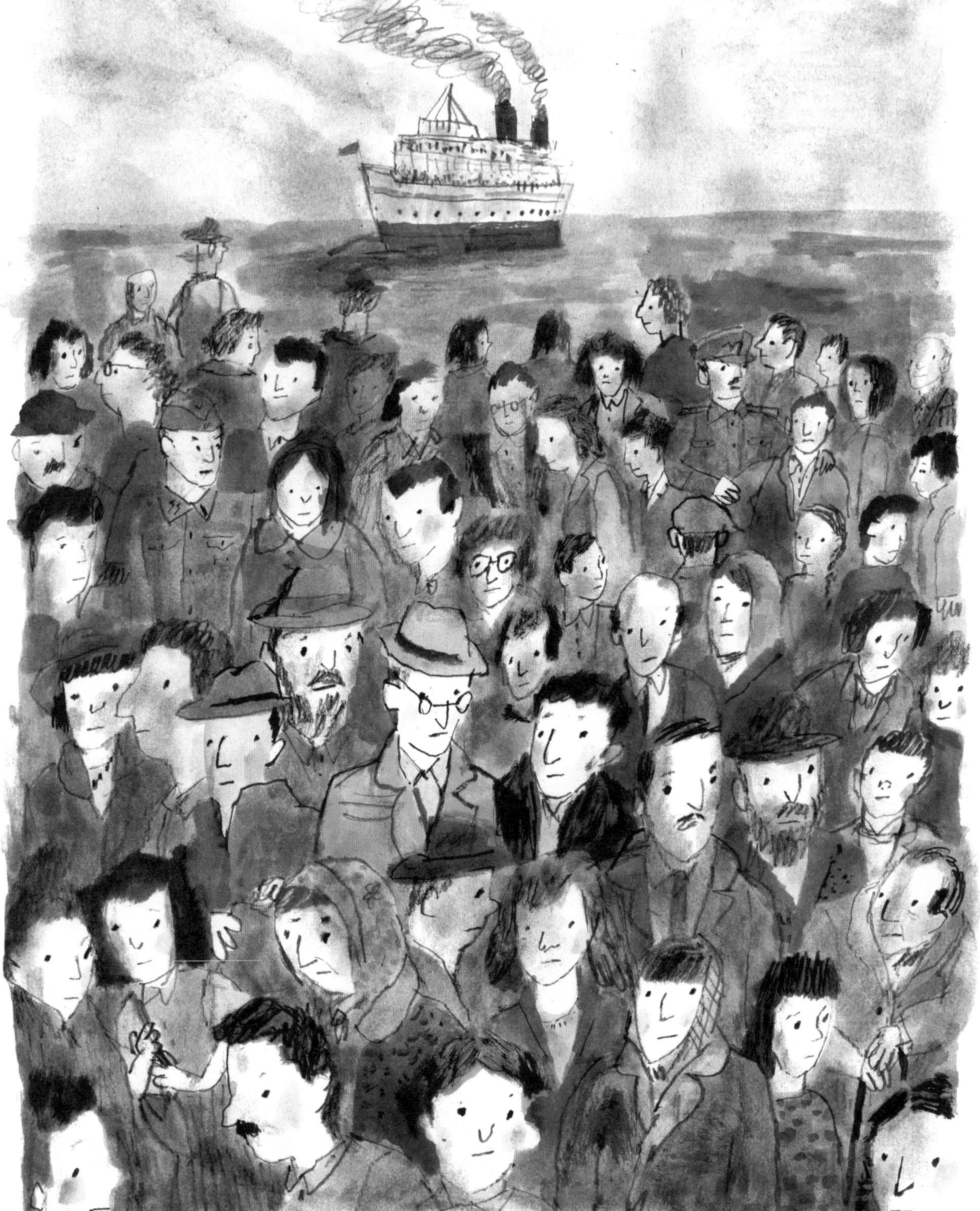

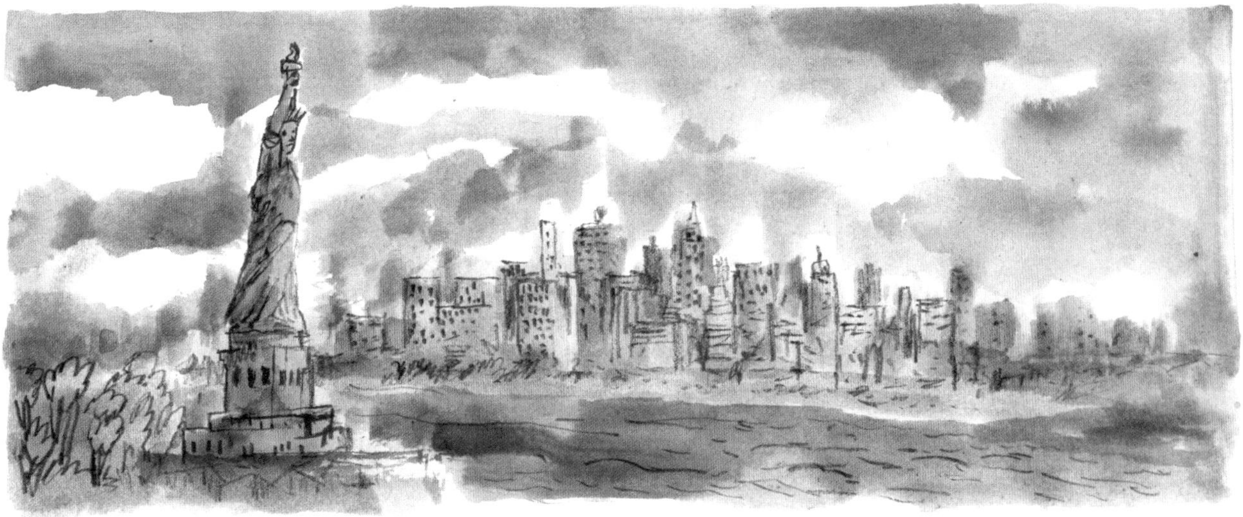

JOE ON THE OTHER HAND... FROM THE FIRST TIME I LAID EYES ON HIM I KNEW HE WAS GOING PLACES.

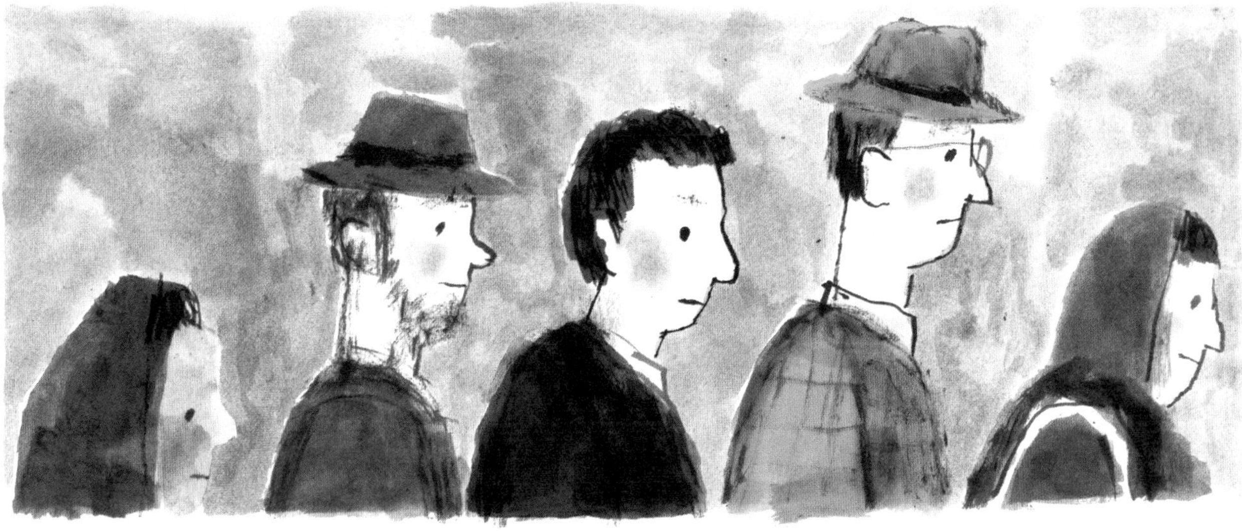

HE WAS AN AMBITIOUS MAN, YOUR ZAYDE JOE.

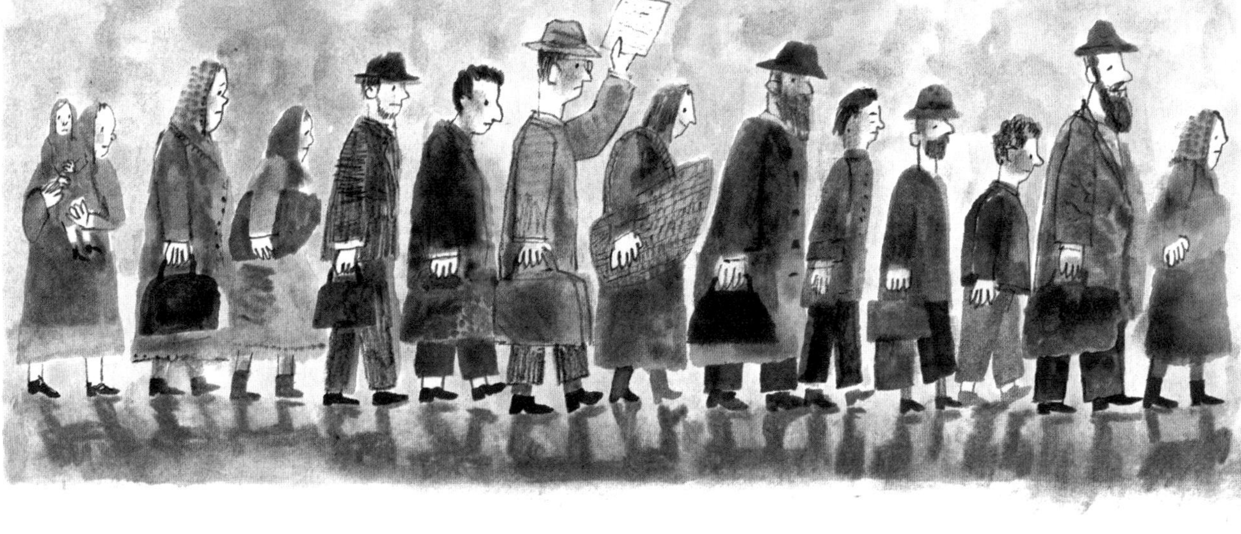

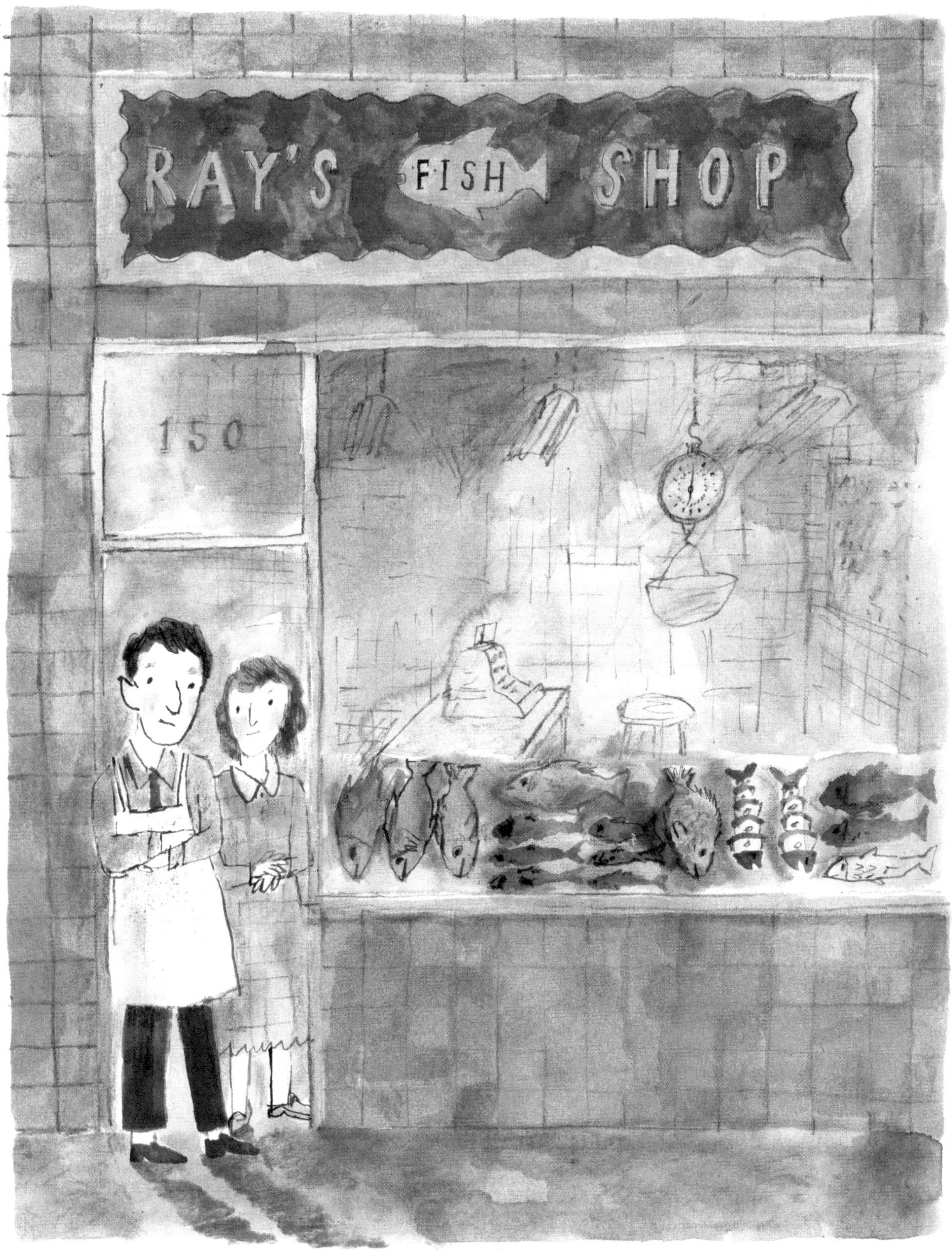
RAY'S FISH SHOP
150

RAY WAS HAPPY WITH HIS LITTLE FISH SHOP. RAY AND ESTI NEVER SEEMED TO CARE THAT THEY DIDN'T HAVE ANY MONEY.

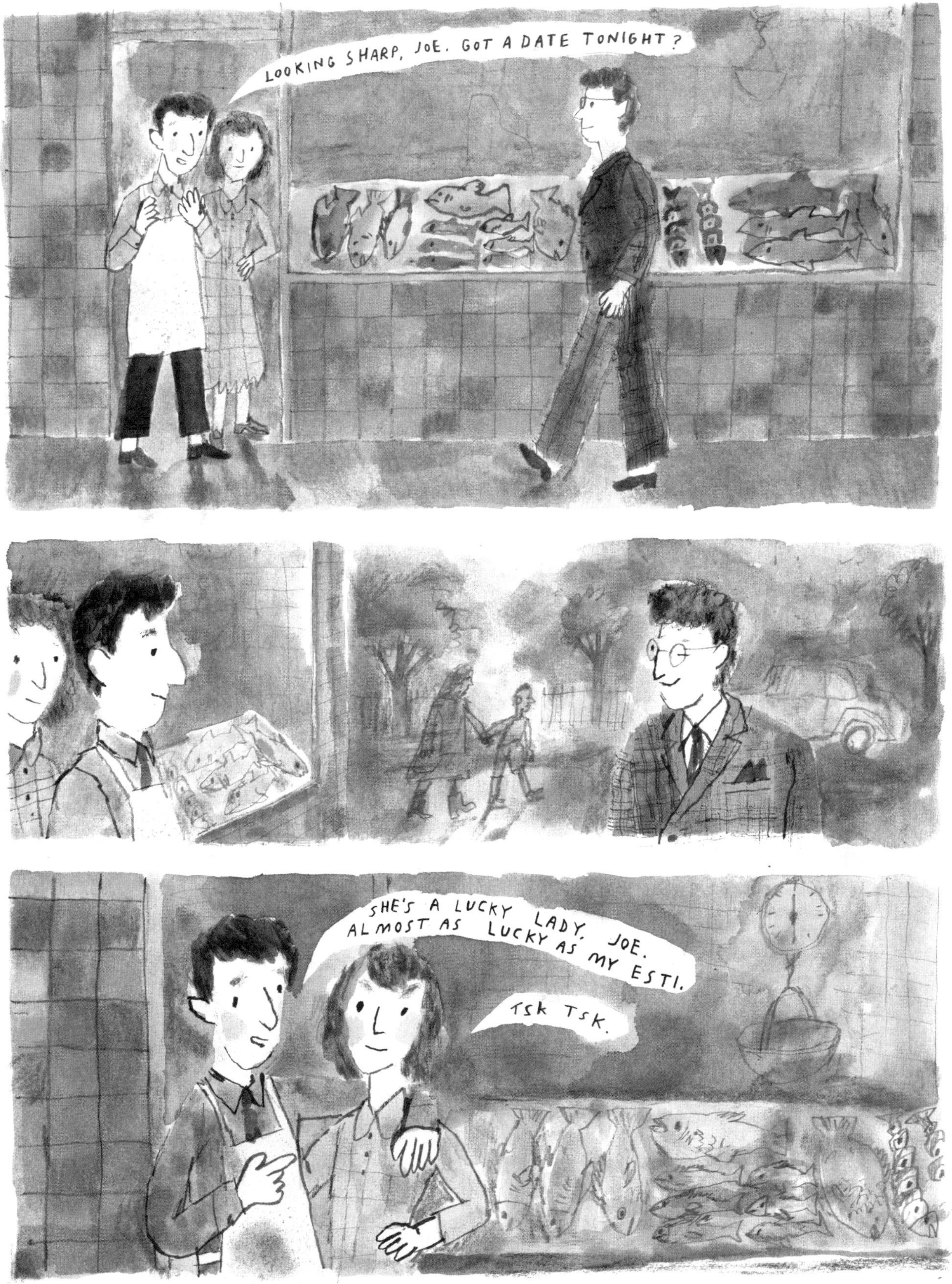
LOOKING SHARP, JOE. GOT A DATE TONIGHT?
SHE'S A LUCKY LADY, JOE. ALMOST AS LUCKY AS MY ESTI.
TSK TSK.

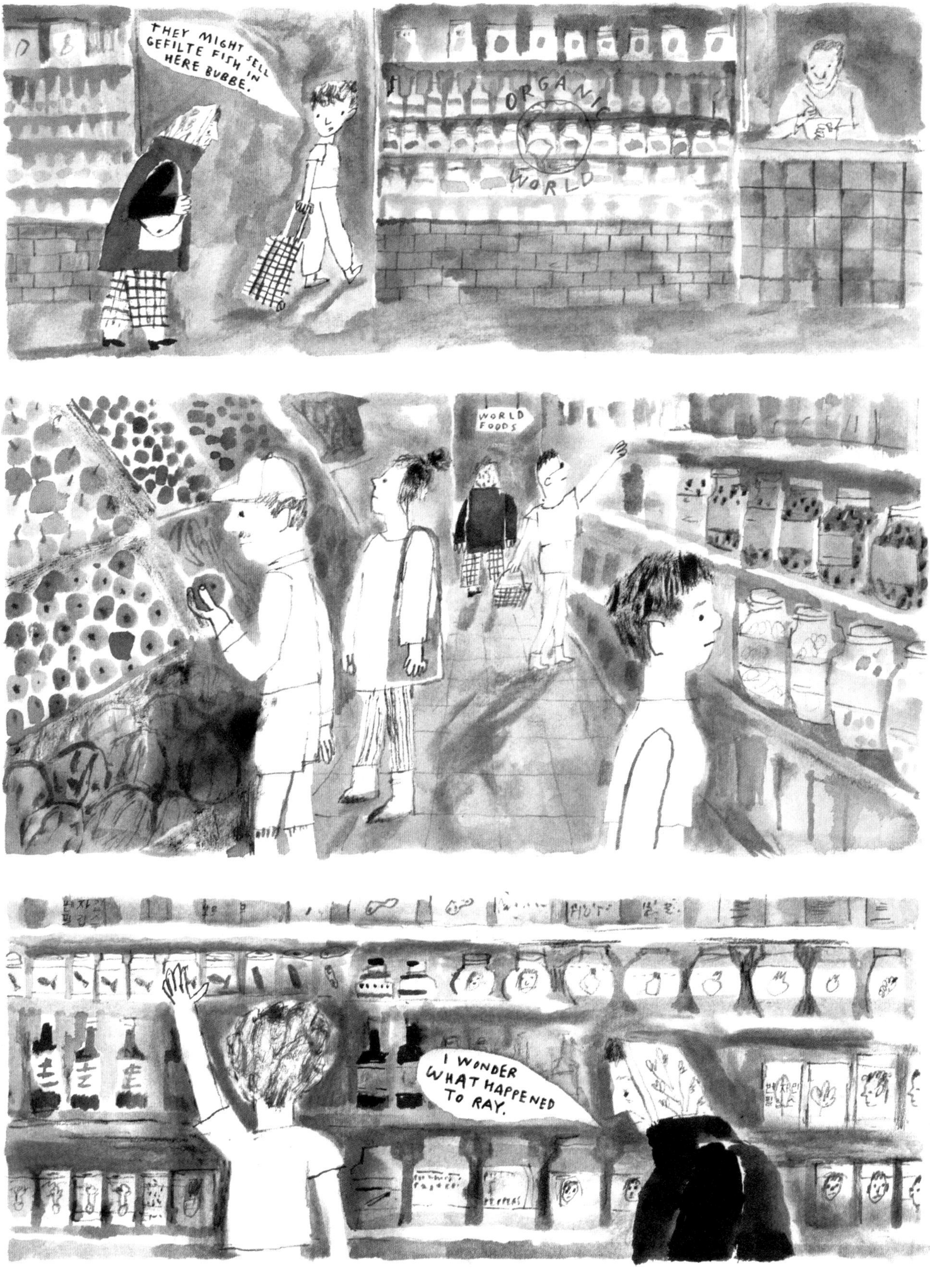
THEY MIGHT SELL GEFILTE FISH IN HERE BUBBE.
ORGANIC WORLD
WORLD FOODS
I WONDER WHAT HAPPENED TO RAY.

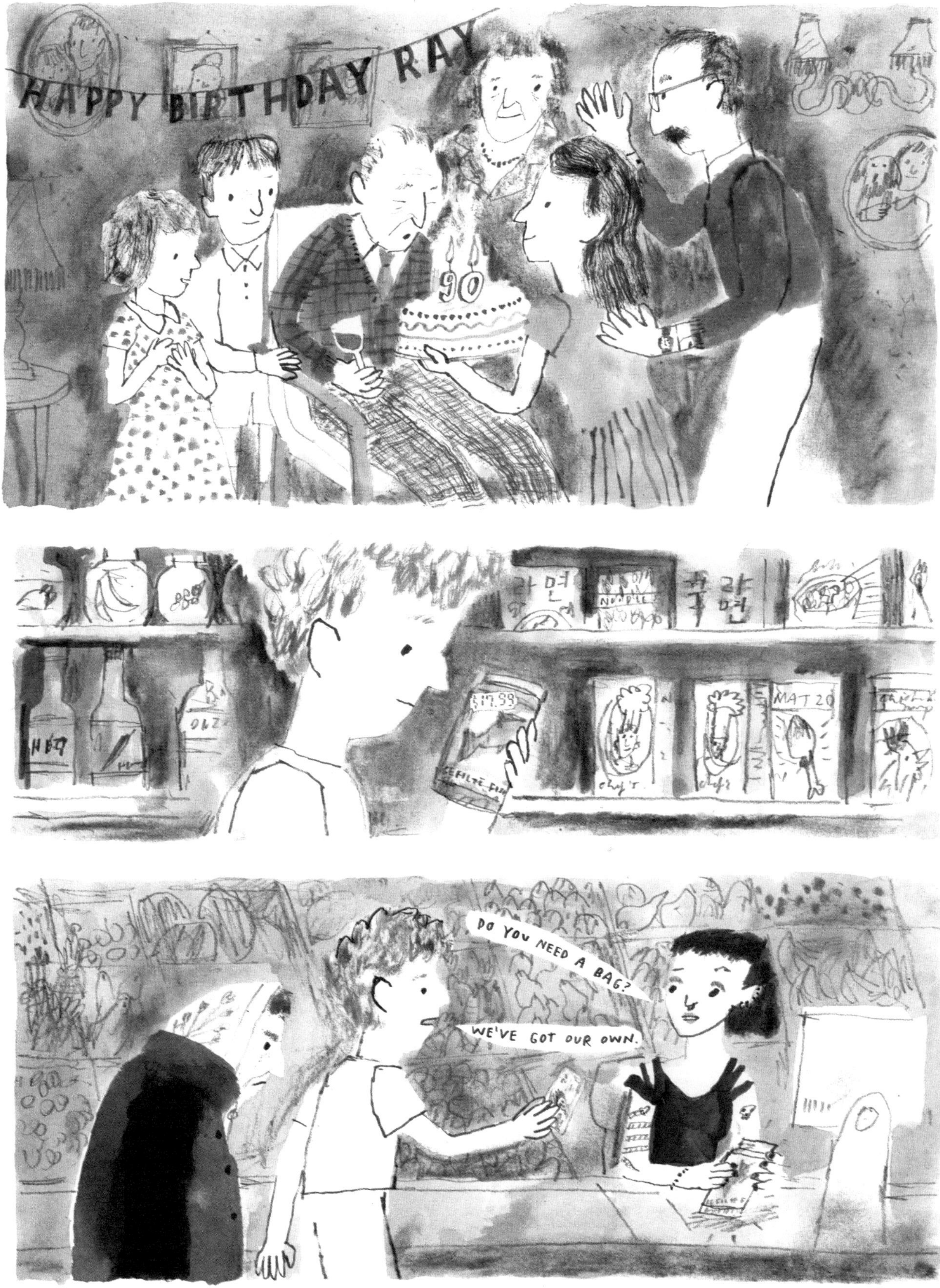
HAPPY BIRTHDAY RAY
90
$17.99
MATZO
DO YOU NEED A BAG?
WE'VE GOT OUR OWN.

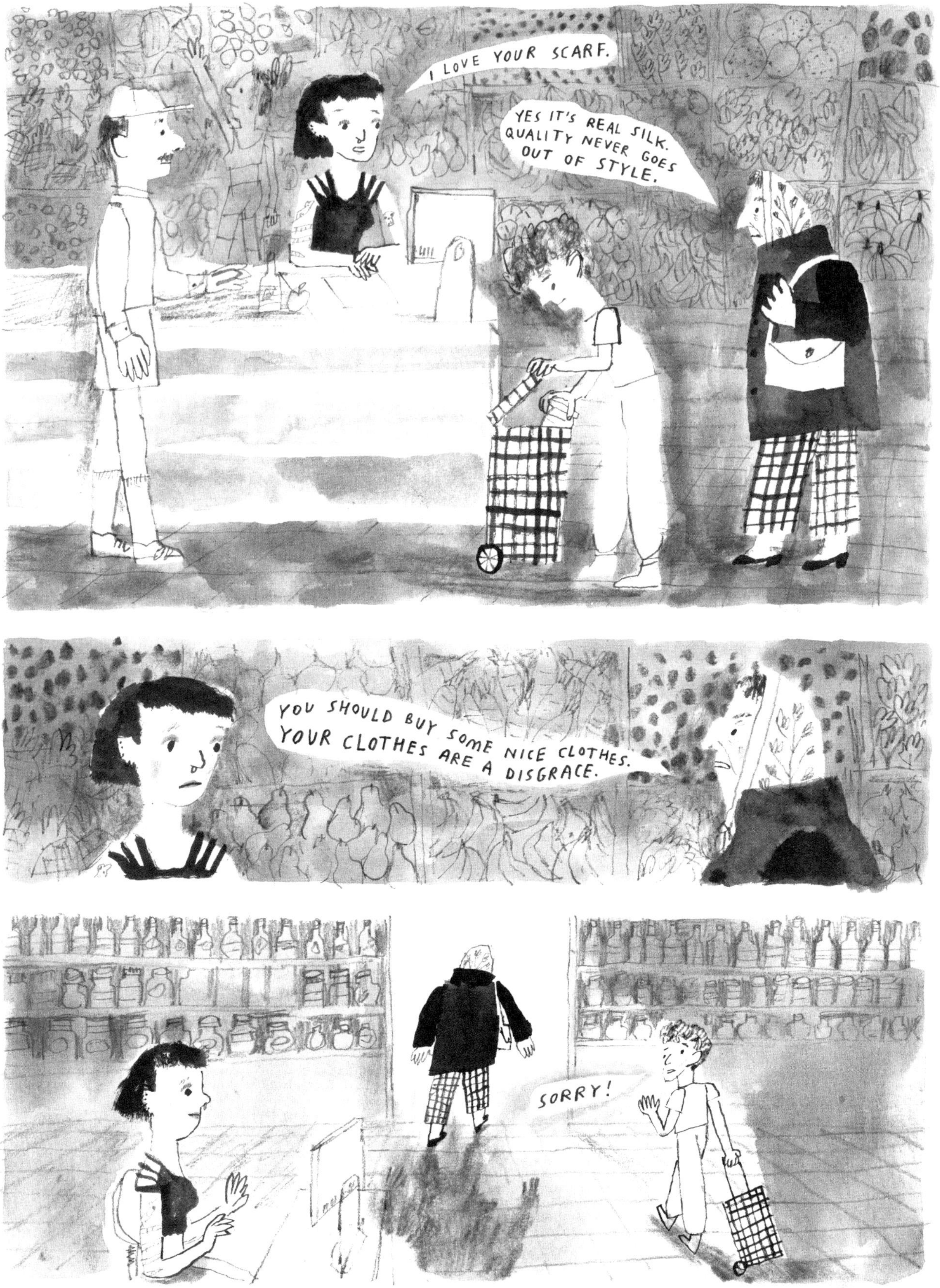
I LOVE YOUR SCARF.
YES IT'S REAL SILK. QUALITY NEVER GOES OUT OF STYLE.
YOU SHOULD BUY SOME NICE CLOTHES. YOUR CLOTHES ARE A DISGRACE.
SORRY!

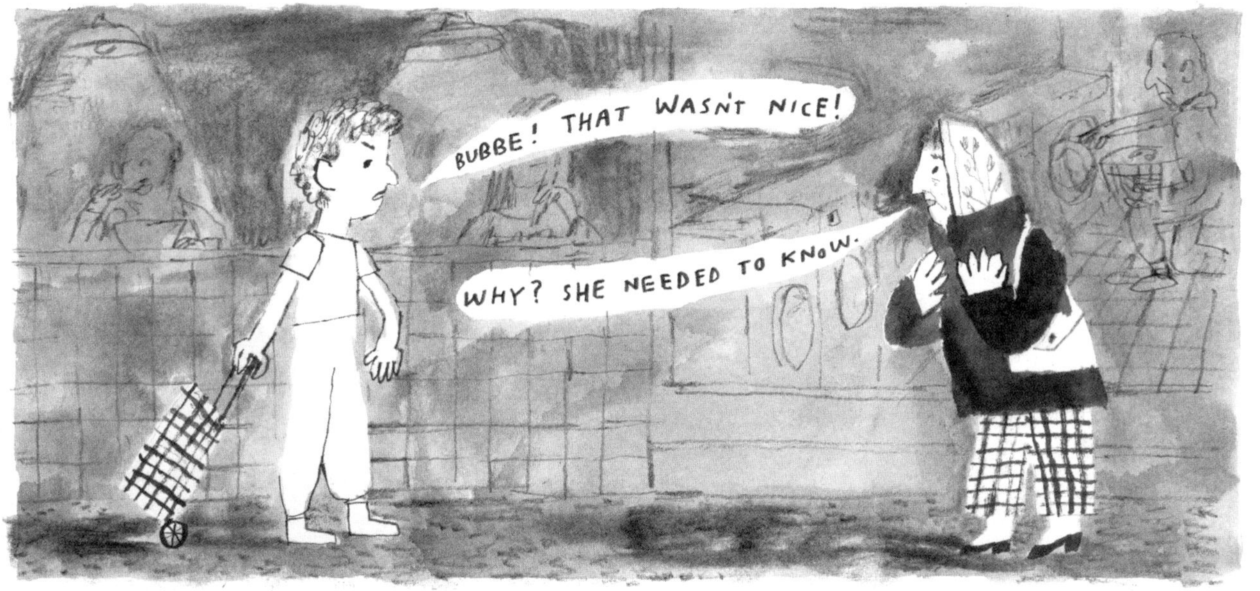
BUBBE! THAT WASN'T NICE!
WHY? SHE NEEDED TO KNOW.

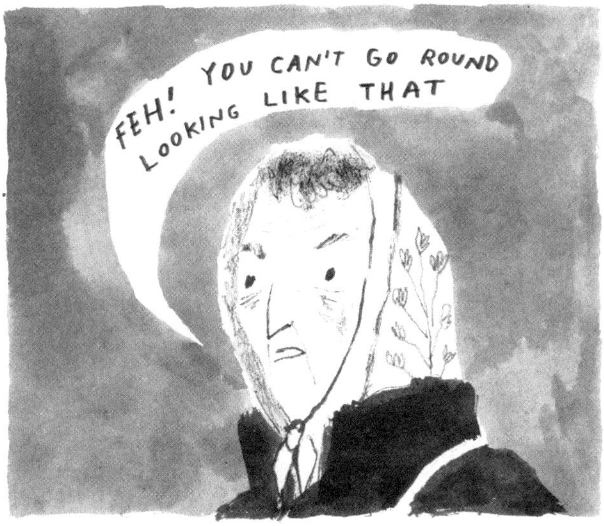
FEH! YOU CAN'T GO ROUND LOOKING LIKE THAT

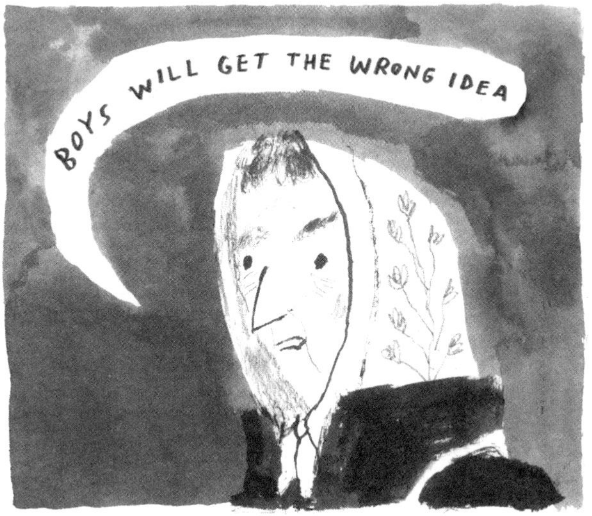
BOYS WILL GET THE WRONG IDEA

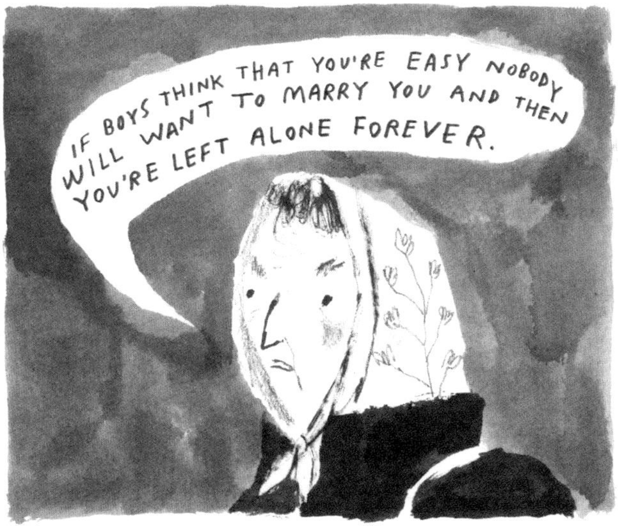
IF BOYS THINK THAT YOU'RE EASY NOBODY WILL WANT TO MARRY YOU AND THEN YOU'RE LEFT ALONE FOREVER.

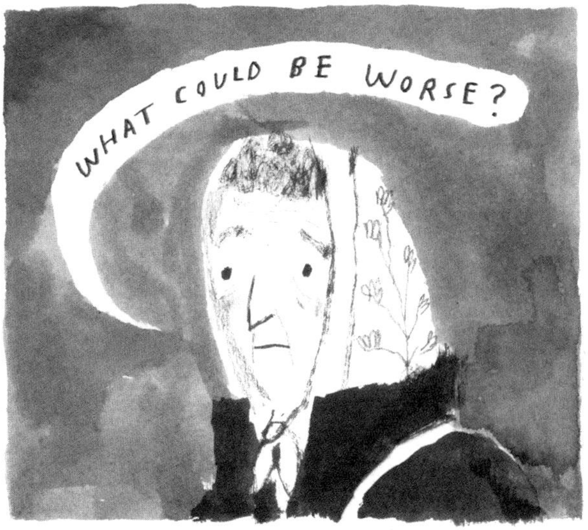
WHAT COULD BE WORSE?

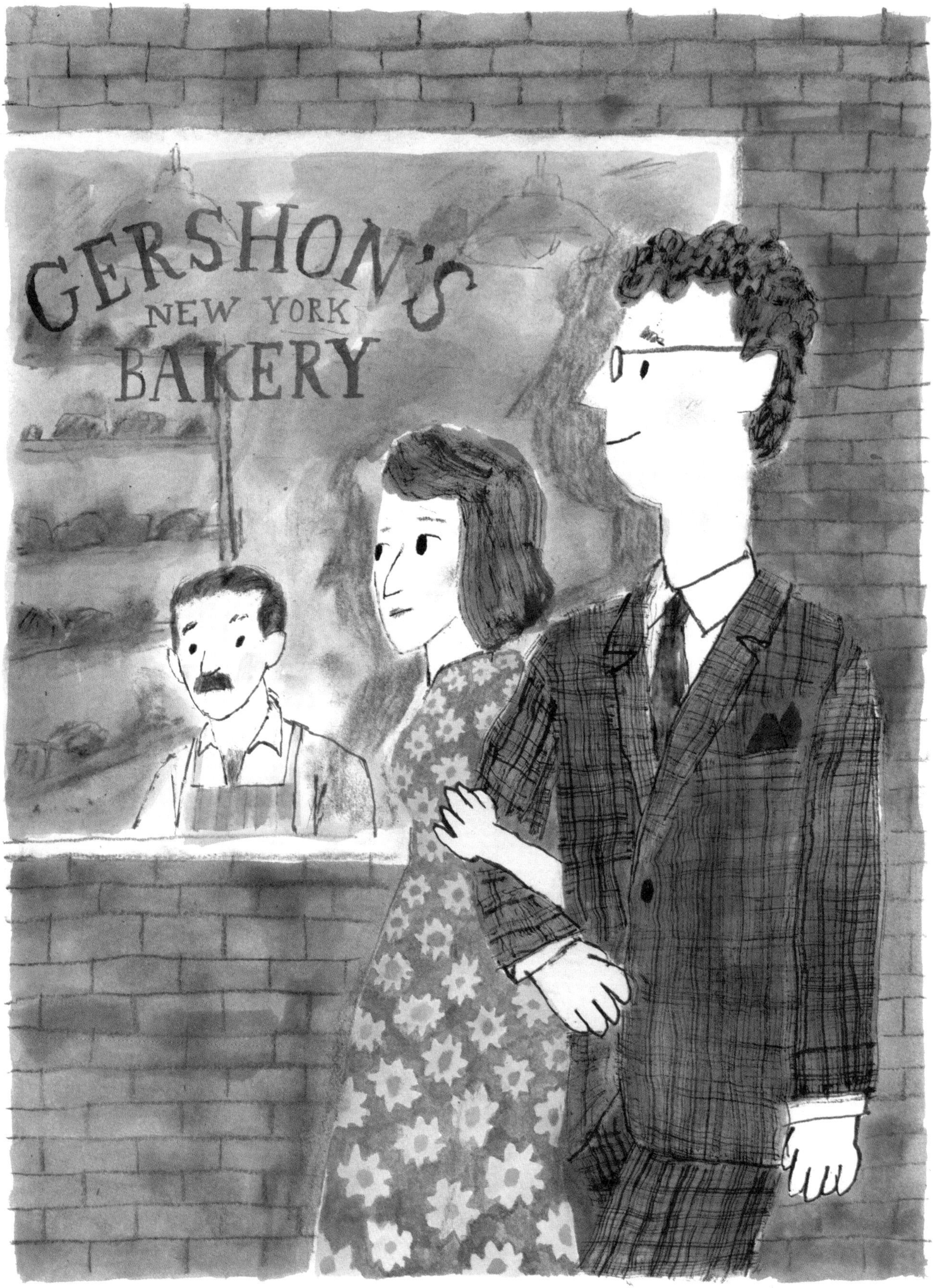
GERSHON'S
NEW YORK
BAKERY

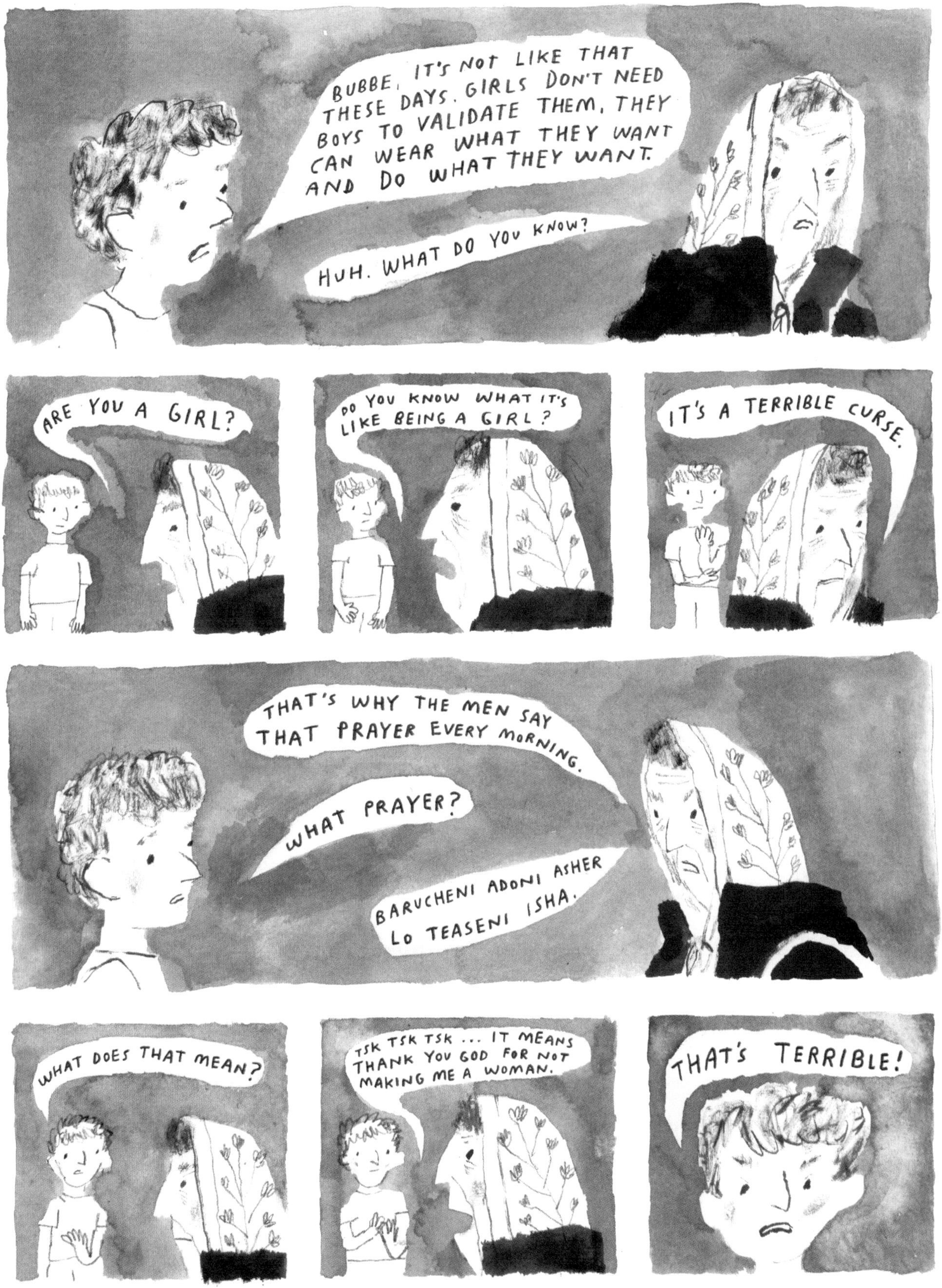
BUBBE, IT'S NOT LIKE THAT THESE DAYS. GIRLS DON'T NEED BOYS TO VALIDATE THEM, THEY CAN WEAR WHAT THEY WANT AND DO WHAT THEY WANT.
HUH. WHAT DO YOU KNOW?
ARE YOU A GIRL?
DO YOU KNOW WHAT IT'S LIKE BEING A GIRL?
IT'S A TERRIBLE CURSE.
THAT'S WHY THE MEN SAY THAT PRAYER EVERY MORNING.
WHAT PRAYER?
BARUCHENI ADONI ASHER LO TEASENI ISHA.
WHAT DOES THAT MEAN?
TSK TSK TSK ... IT MEANS THANK YOU GOD FOR NOT MAKING ME A WOMAN.
THAT'S TERRIBLE!

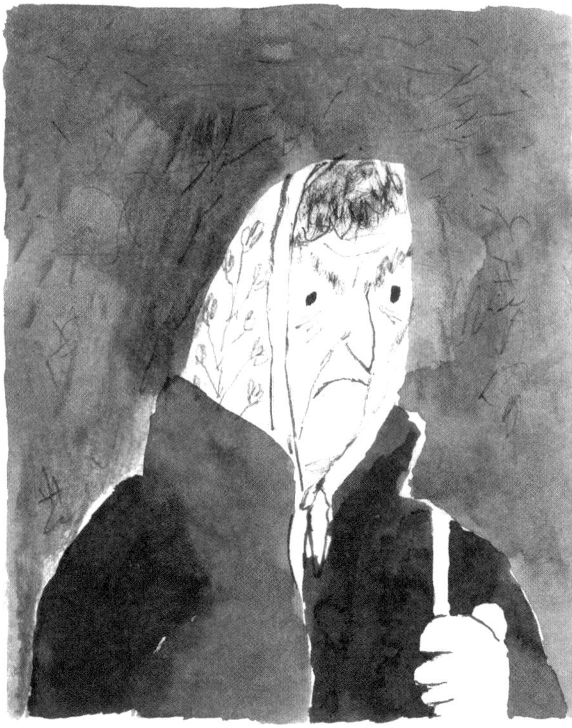

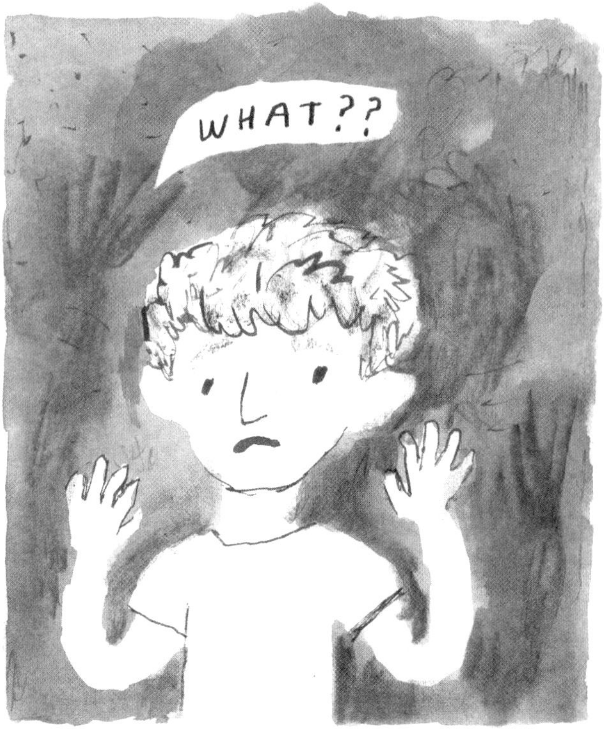
WHAT??

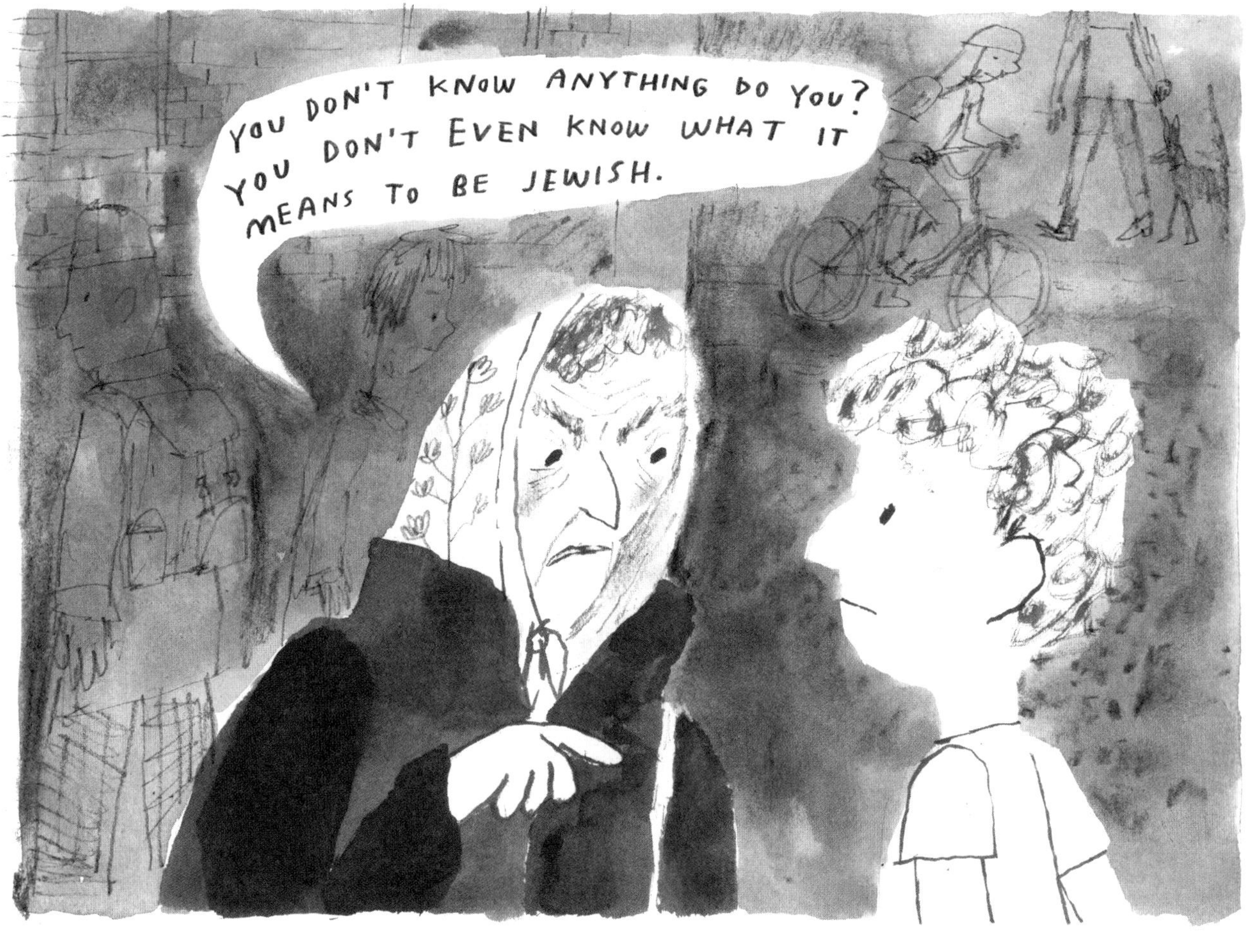
YOU DON'T KNOW ANYTHING DO YOU? YOU DON'T EVEN KNOW WHAT IT MEANS TO BE JEWISH.

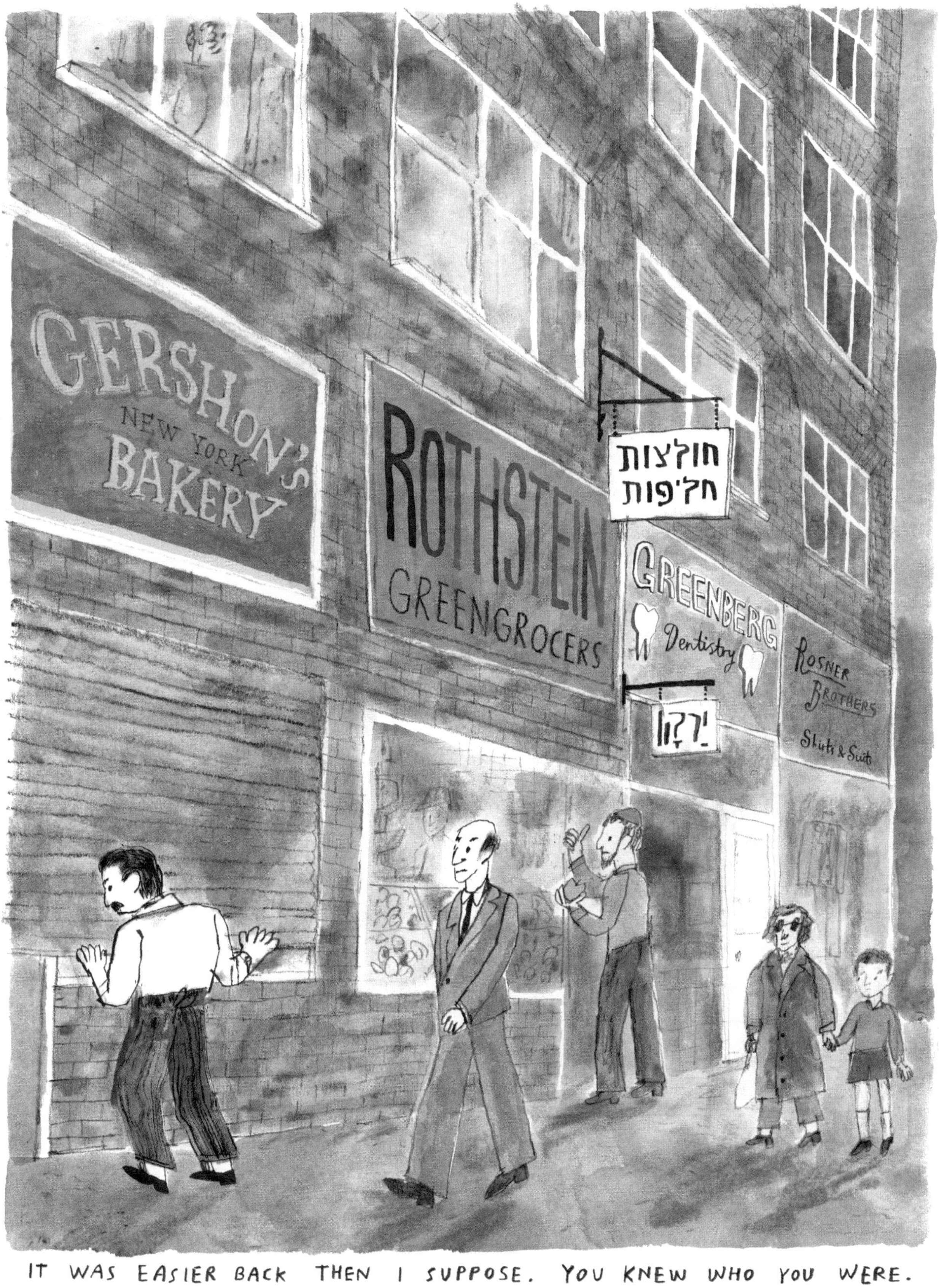
GERSHON'S
NEW YORK
BAKERY
ROTHSTEIN
GREENGROCERS
חולצות
חליפות
GREENBERG
Dentistry
ירקן
ROSNER
BROTHERS
Shirts & Suits

IT WAS EASIER BACK THEN I SUPPOSE. YOU KNEW WHO YOU WERE.

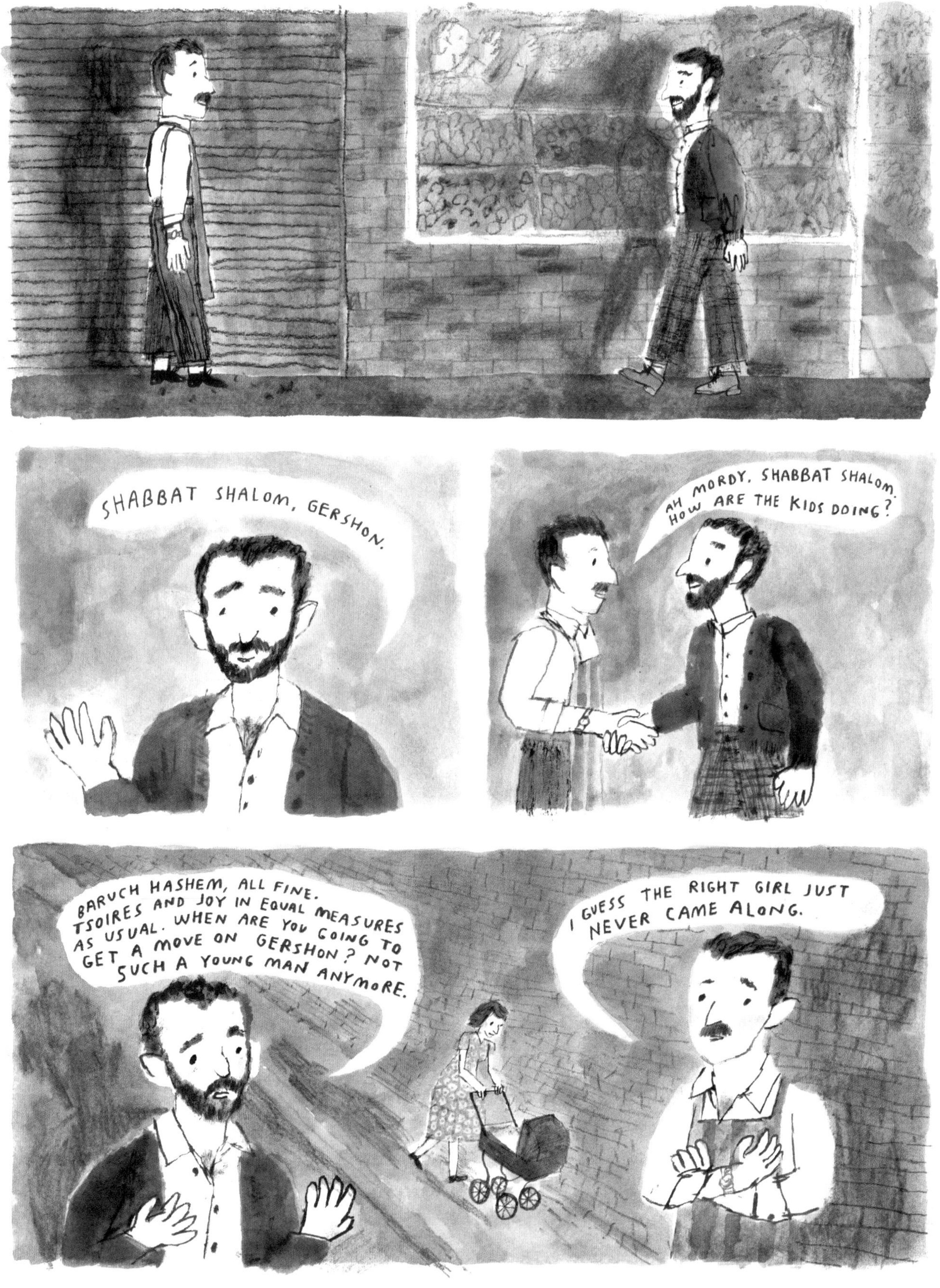
SHABBAT SHALOM, GERSHON.
AH MORDY. SHABBAT SHALOM. HOW ARE THE KIDS DOING?
BARUCH HASHEM, ALL FINE. TSOIRES AND JOY IN EQUAL MEASURES AS USUAL. WHEN ARE YOU GOING TO GET A MOVE ON GERSHON? NOT SUCH A YOUNG MAN ANYMORE.
I GUESS THE RIGHT GIRL JUST NEVER CAME ALONG.

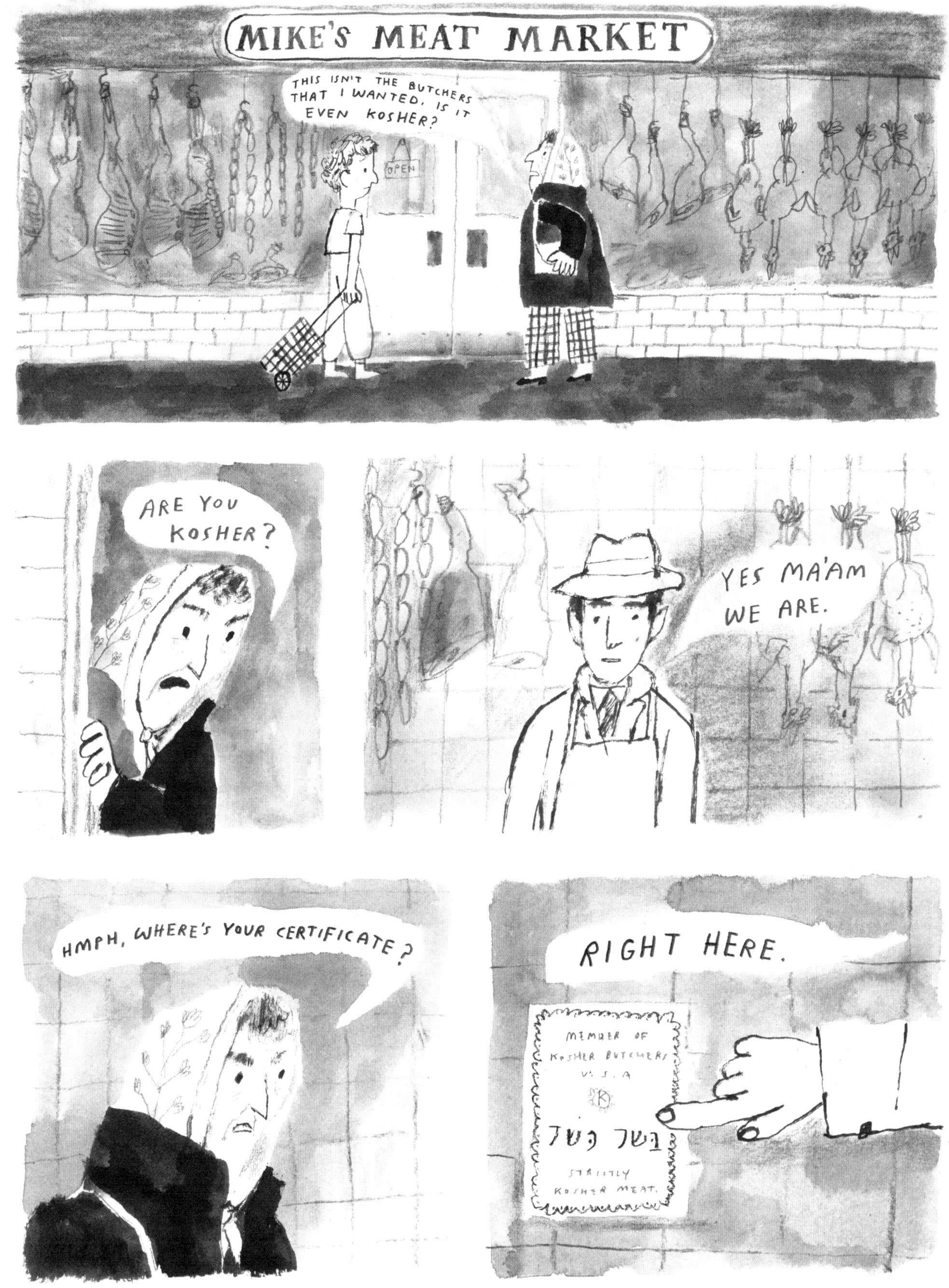
MIKE'S MEAT MARKET
THIS ISN'T THE BUTCHERS THAT I WANTED, IS IT EVEN KOSHER?
OPEN
ARE YOU KOSHER?
YES MA'AM WE ARE.
HMPH, WHERE'S YOUR CERTIFICATE?
RIGHT HERE.
MEMBER OF KOSHER BUTCHERS U.S.A
STRICTLY KOSHER MEAT.

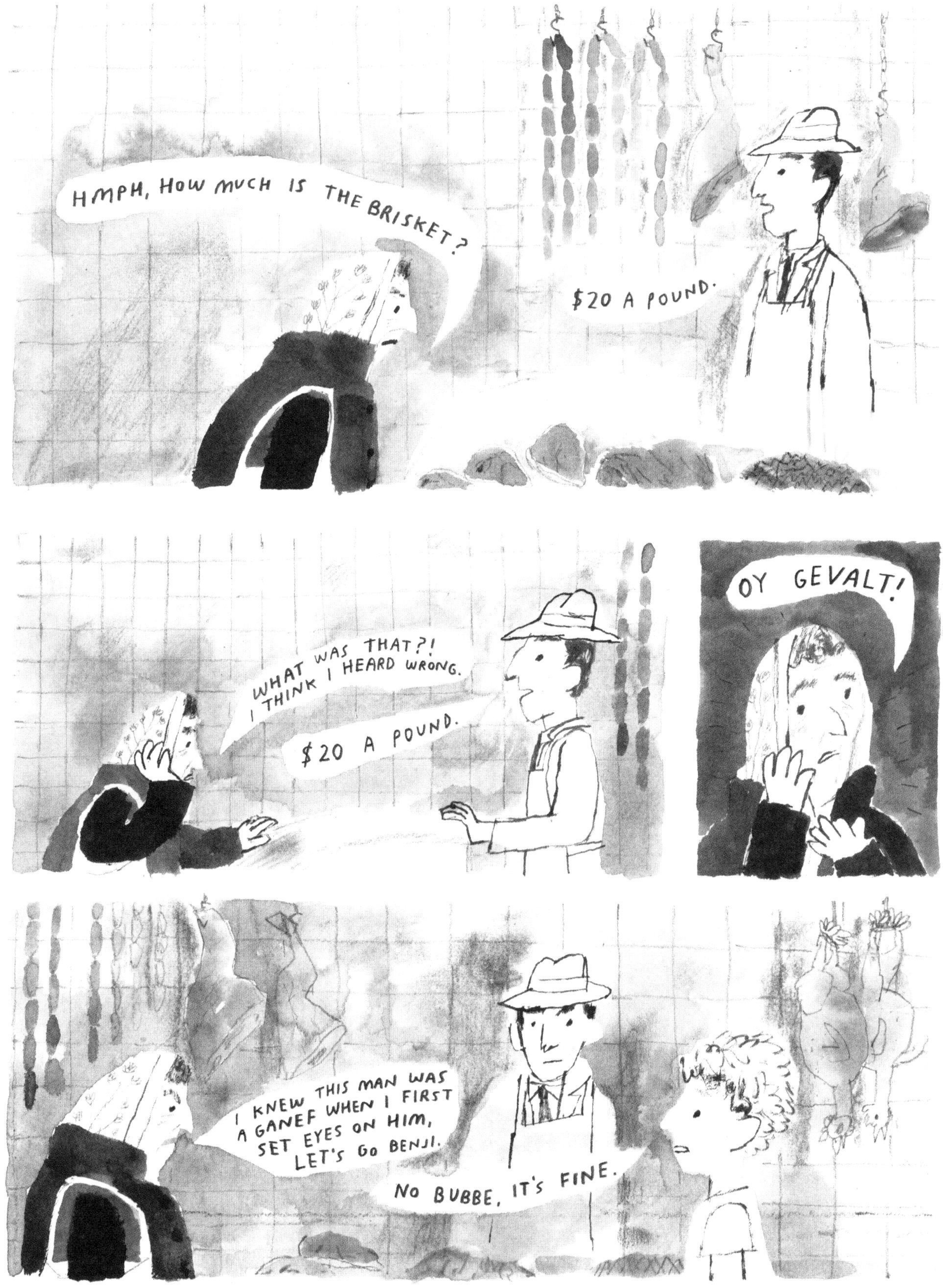
HMPH, HOW MUCH IS THE BRISKET?
$20 A POUND.
WHAT WAS THAT?! I THINK I HEARD WRONG.
$20 A POUND.
OY GEVALT!
I KNEW THIS MAN WAS A GANEF WHEN I FIRST SET EYES ON HIM, LET'S GO BENJI.
NO BUBBE, IT'S FINE.

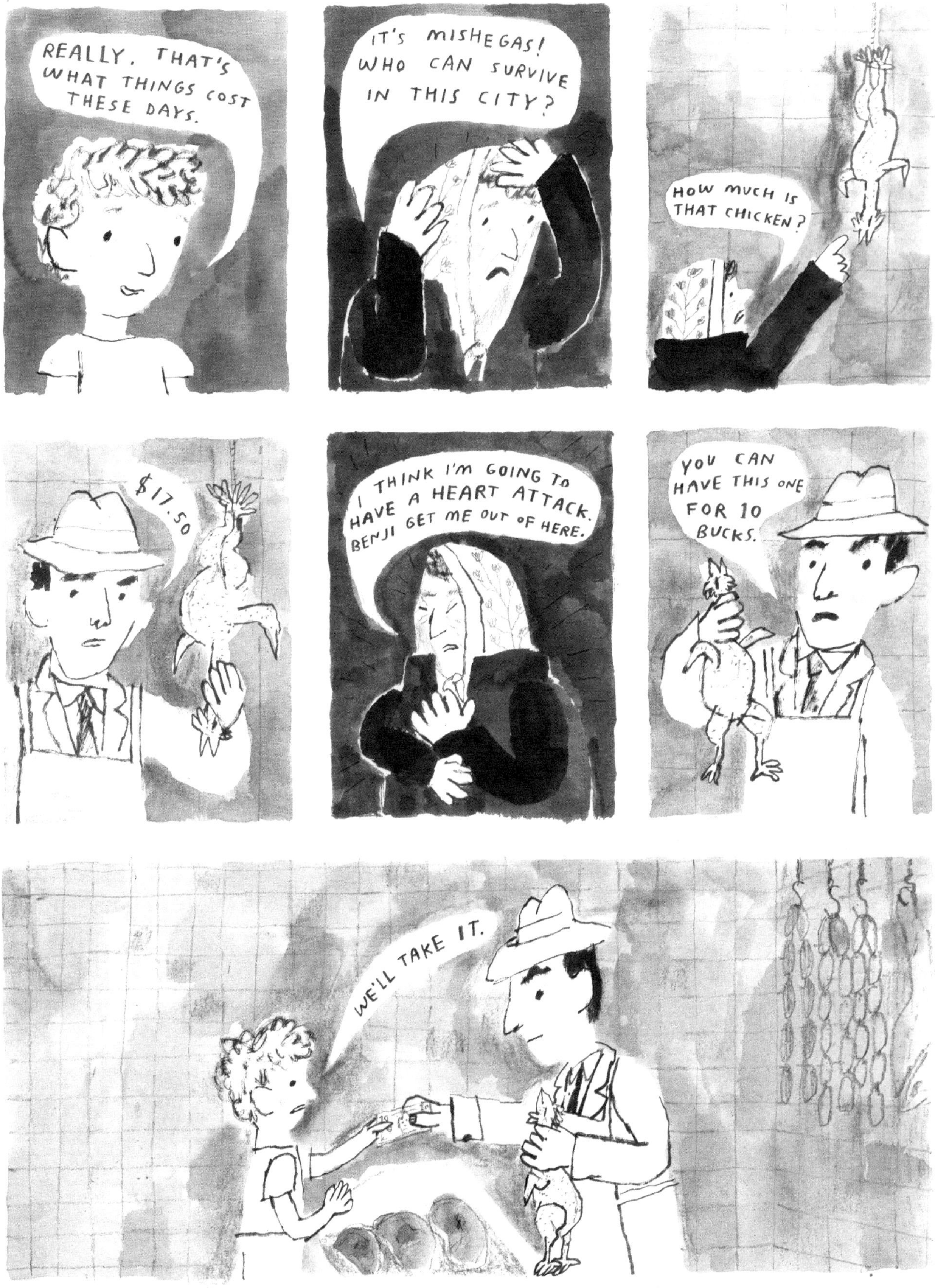
REALLY. THAT'S WHAT THINGS COST THESE DAYS.
IT'S MISHEGAS! WHO CAN SURVIVE IN THIS CITY?
HOW MUCH IS THAT CHICKEN?
$17.50
I THINK I'M GOING TO HAVE A HEART ATTACK. BENJI GET ME OUT OF HERE.
YOU CAN HAVE THIS ONE FOR 10 BUCKS.
WE'LL TAKE IT.

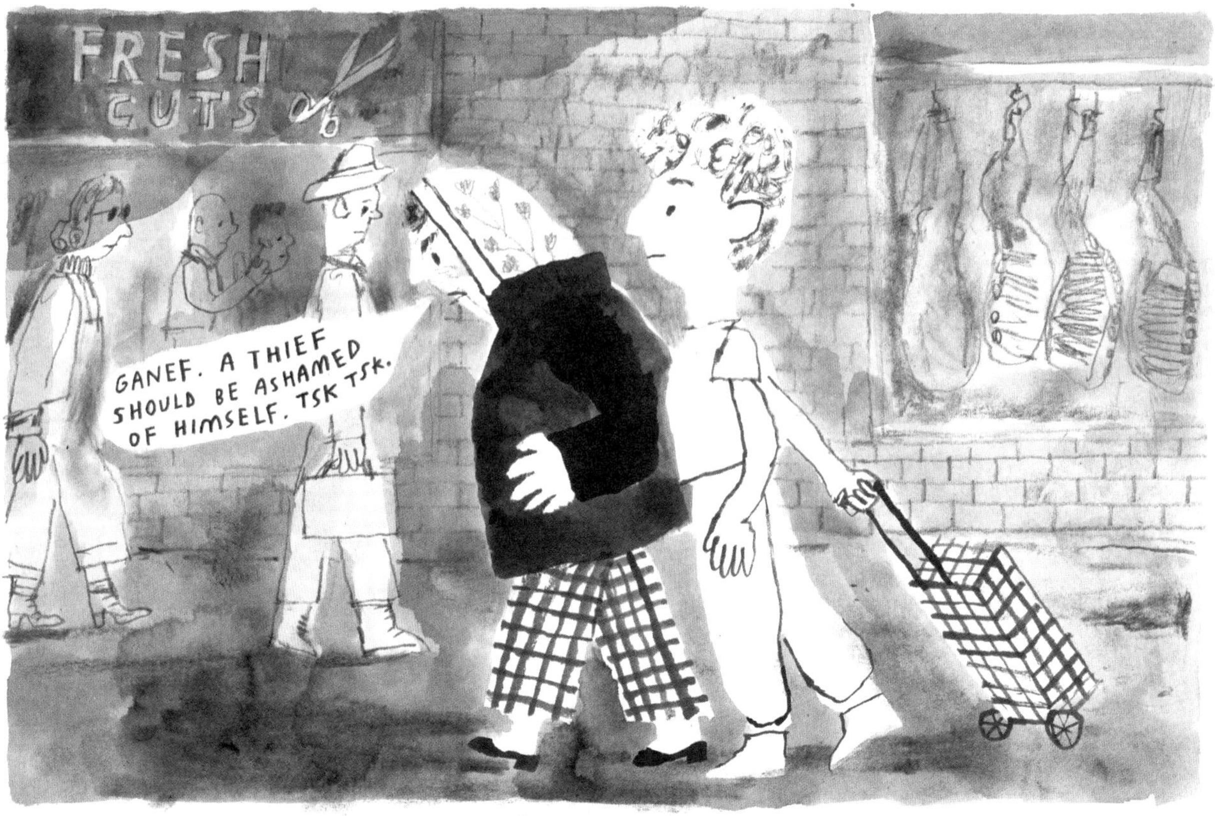
FRESH CUTS
GANEF. A THIEF SHOULD BE ASHAMED OF HIMSELF. TSK TSK.

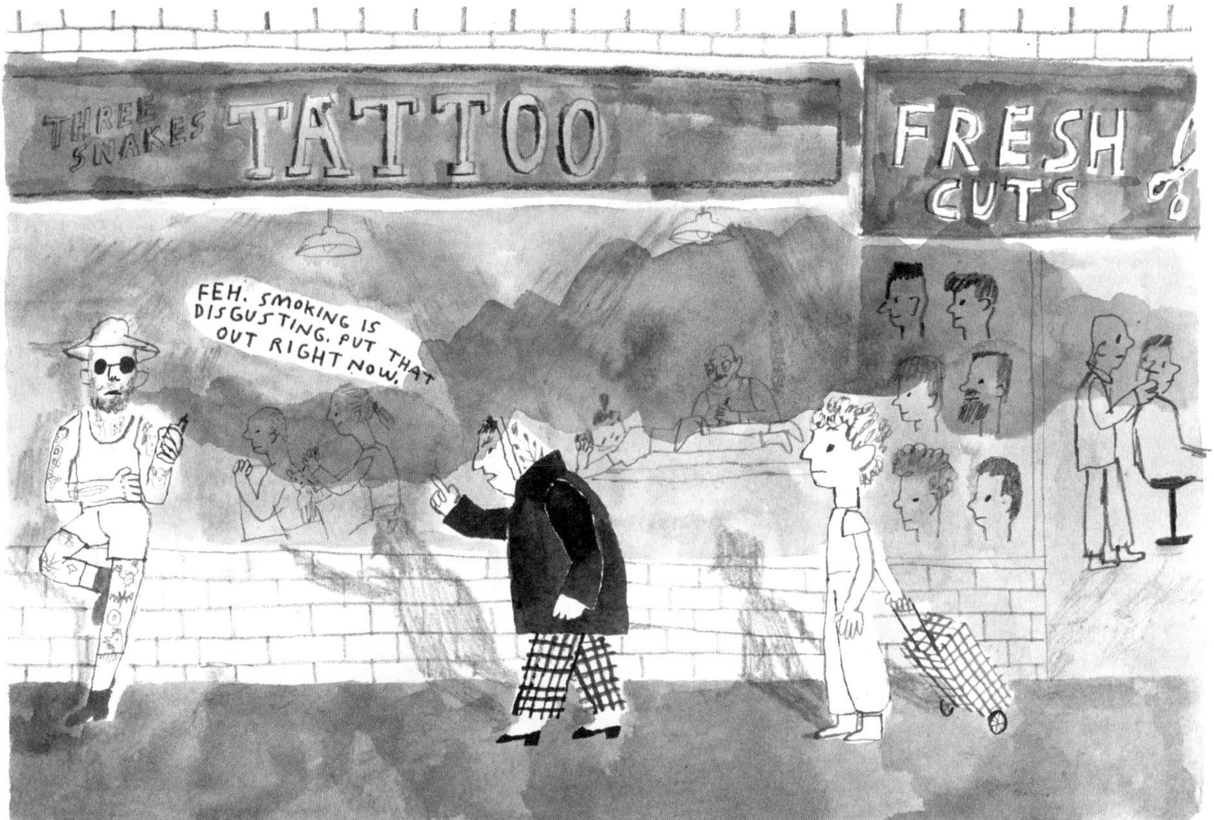
THREE SNAKES TATTOO
FRESH CUTS
FEH. SMOKING IS DISGUSTING. PUT THAT OUT RIGHT NOW.

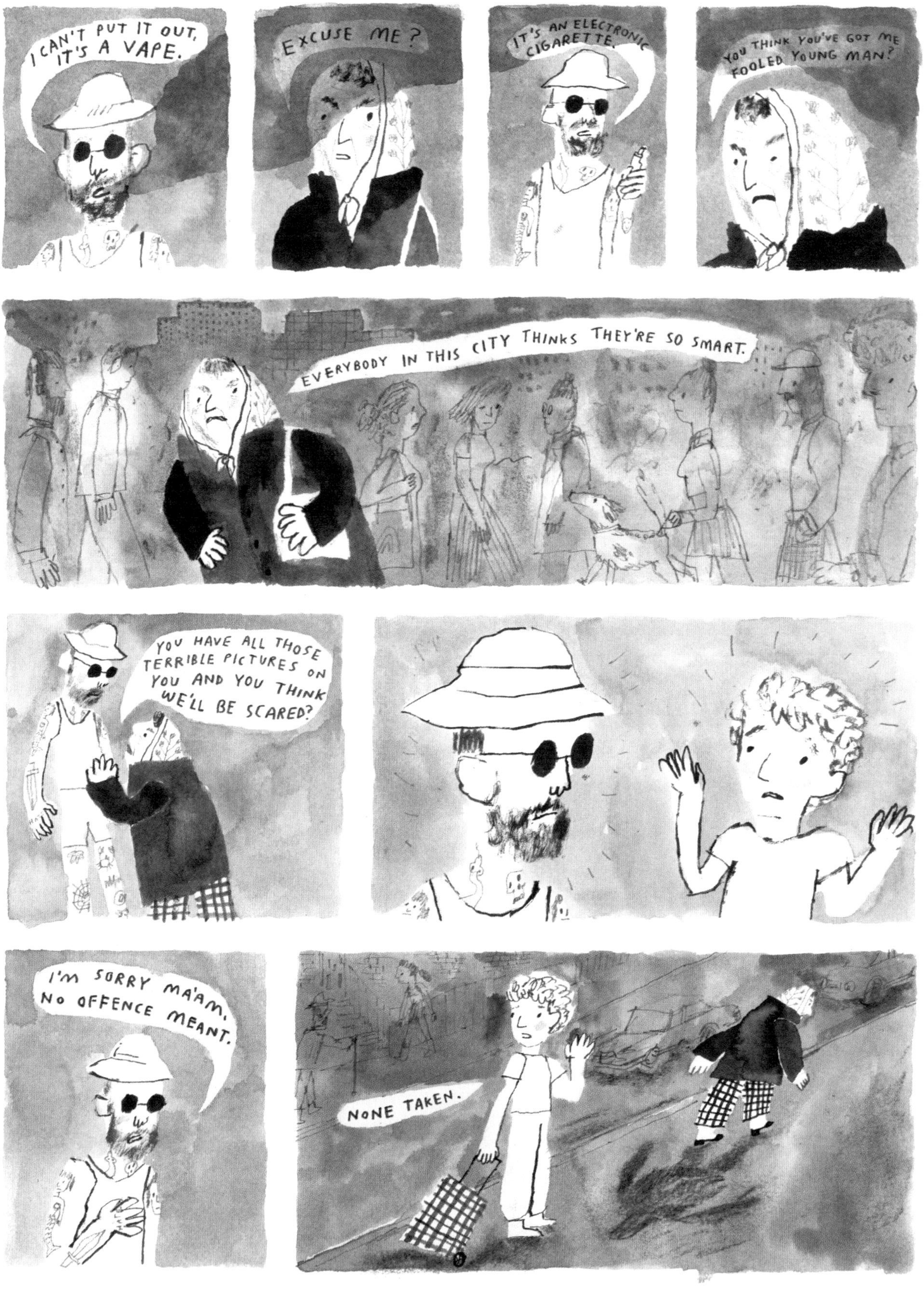
I CAN'T PUT IT OUT, IT'S A VAPE.
EXCUSE ME?
IT'S AN ELECTRONIC CIGARETTE.
YOU THINK YOU'VE GOT ME FOOLED YOUNG MAN?
EVERYBODY IN THIS CITY THINKS THEY'RE SO SMART.
YOU HAVE ALL THOSE TERRIBLE PICTURES ON YOU AND YOU THINK WE'LL BE SCARED?
I'M SORRY MA'AM, NO OFFENCE MEANT.
NONE TAKEN.

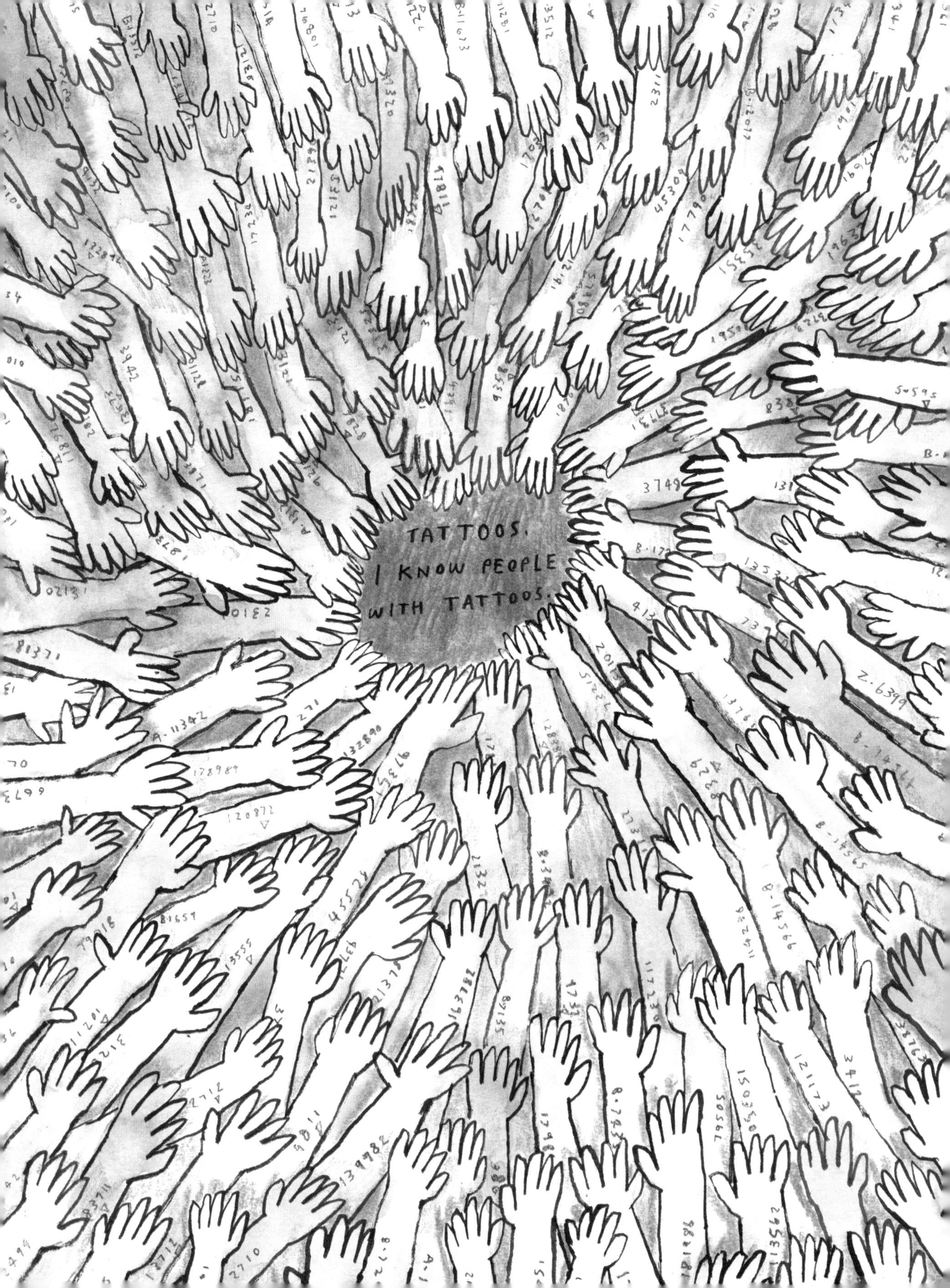
TATTOOS.
I KNOW PEOPLE
WITH TATTOOS.

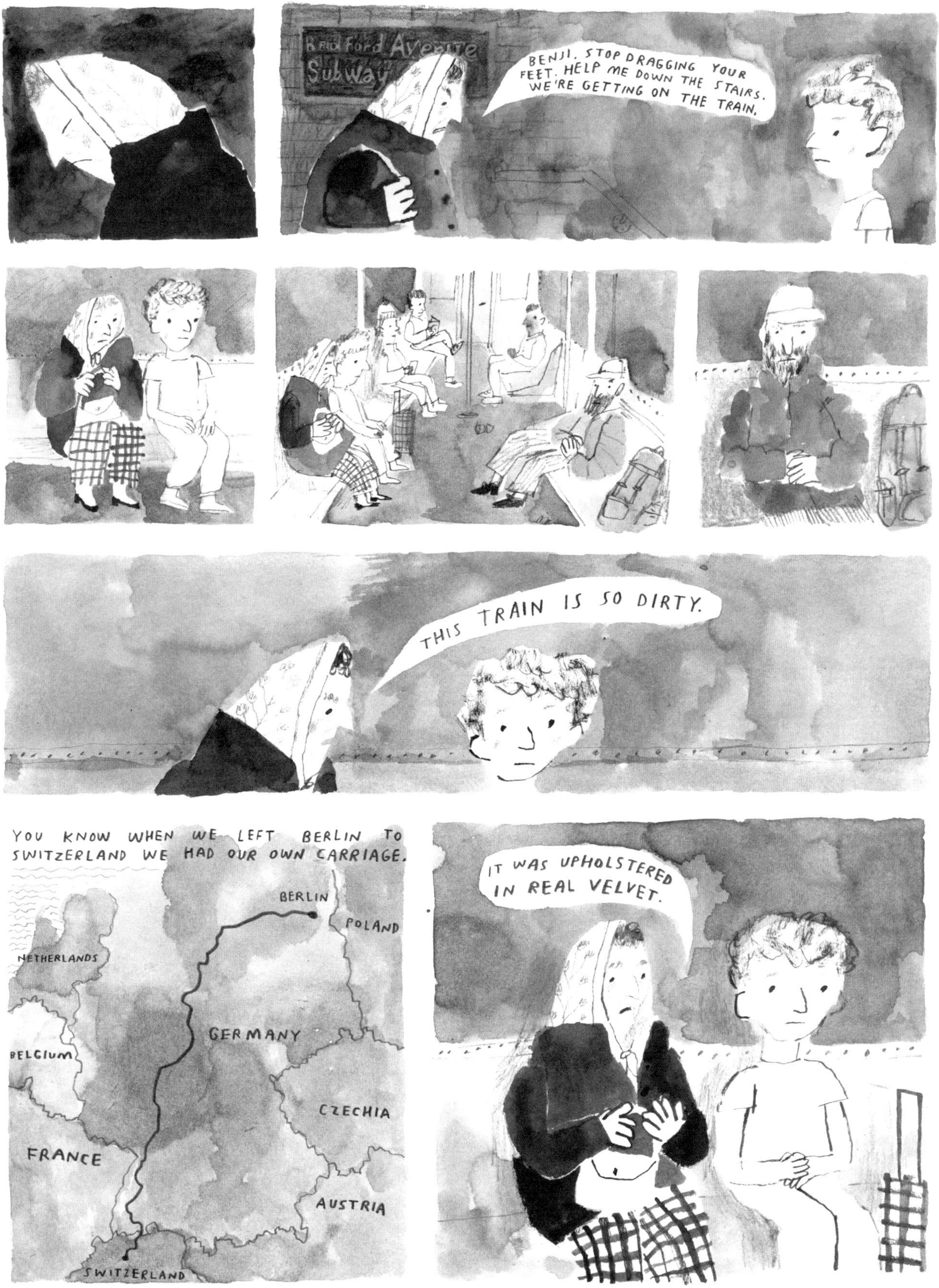
Bedford Avenue Subway
BENJI, STOP DRAGGING YOUR FEET. HELP ME DOWN THE STAIRS. WE'RE GETTING ON THE TRAIN.
THIS TRAIN IS SO DIRTY.
YOU KNOW WHEN WE LEFT BERLIN TO SWITZERLAND WE HAD OUR OWN CARRIAGE.
BERLIN
POLAND
NETHERLANDS
BELGIUM
GERMANY
CZECHIA
FRANCE
AUSTRIA
SWITZERLAND
IT WAS UPHOLSTERED IN REAL VELVET.

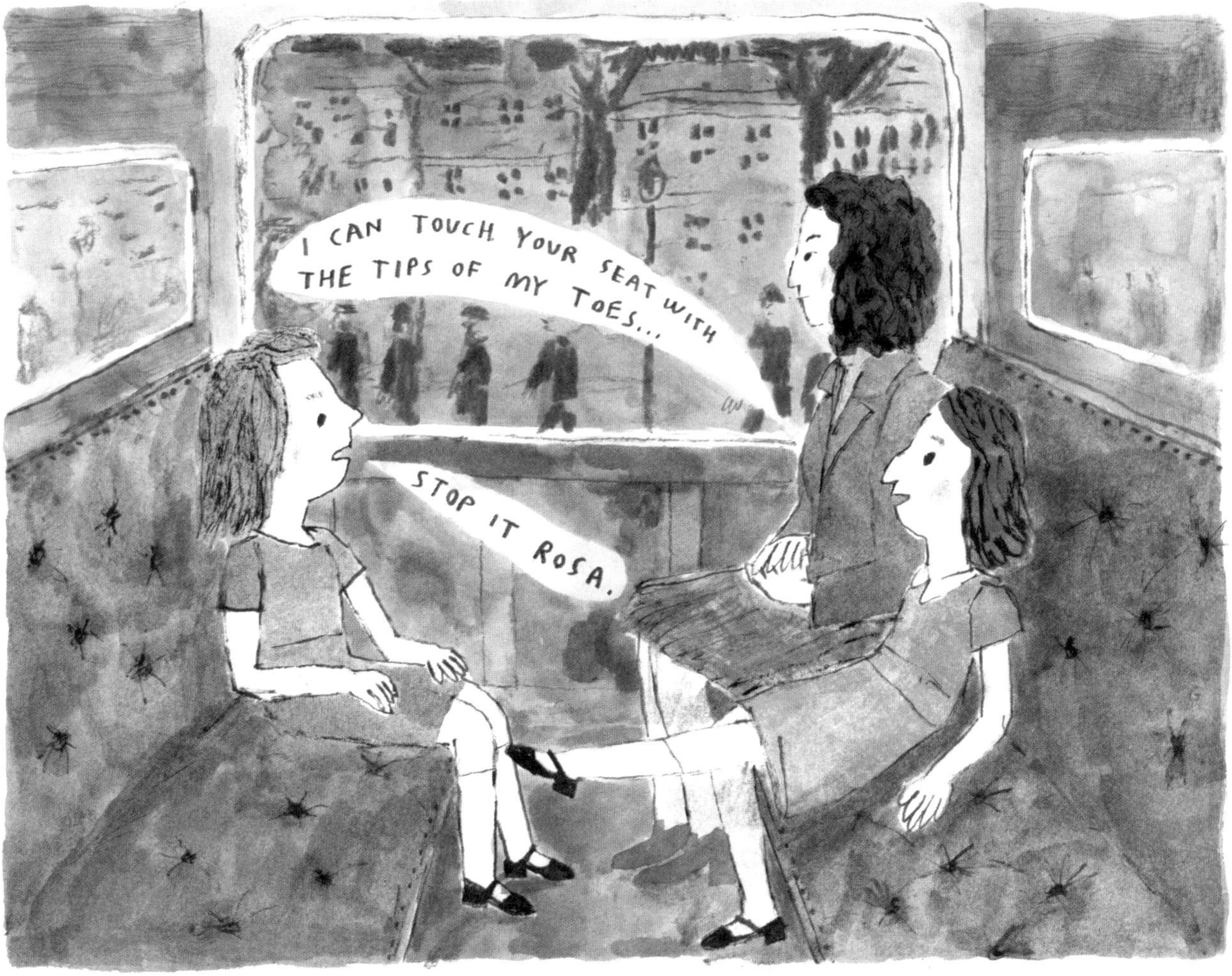
I CAN TOUCH YOUR SEAT WITH THE TIPS OF MY TOES...
STOP IT ROSA.

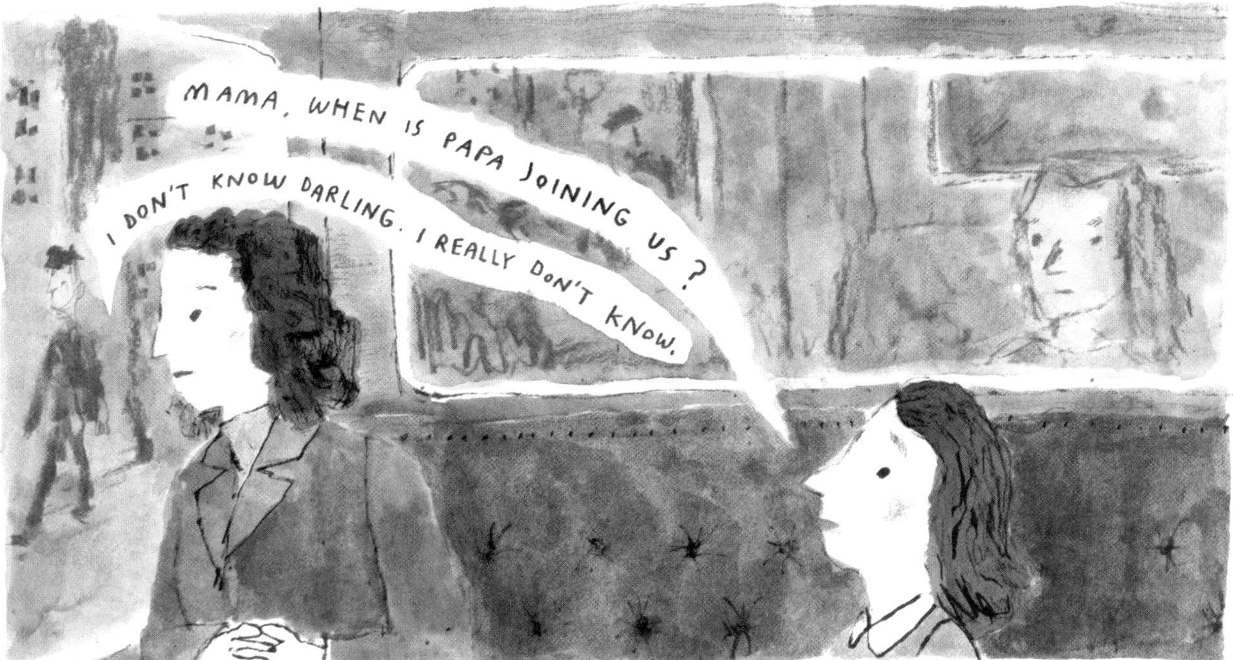
MAMA, WHEN IS PAPA JOINING US?
I DON'T KNOW DARLING. I REALLY DON'T KNOW.

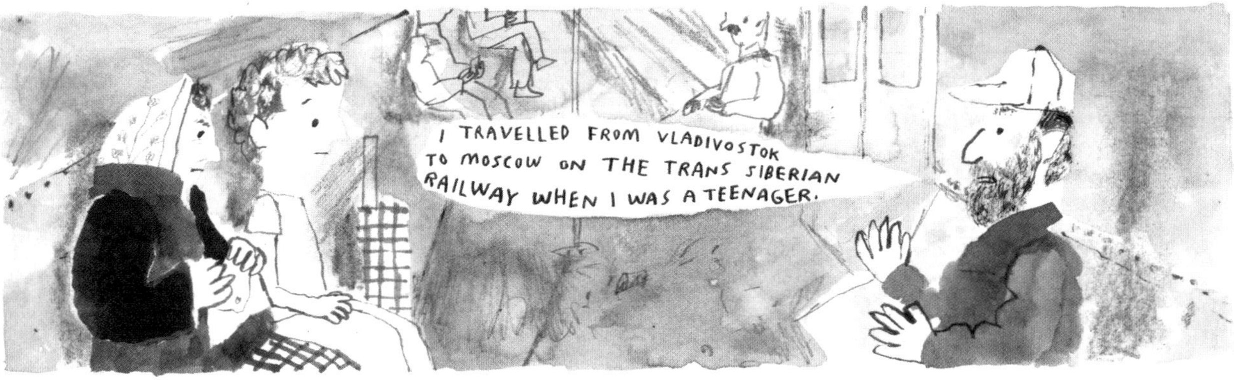
I TRAVELLED FROM VLADIVOSTOK TO MOSCOW ON THE TRANS SIBERIAN RAILWAY WHEN I WAS A TEENAGER.

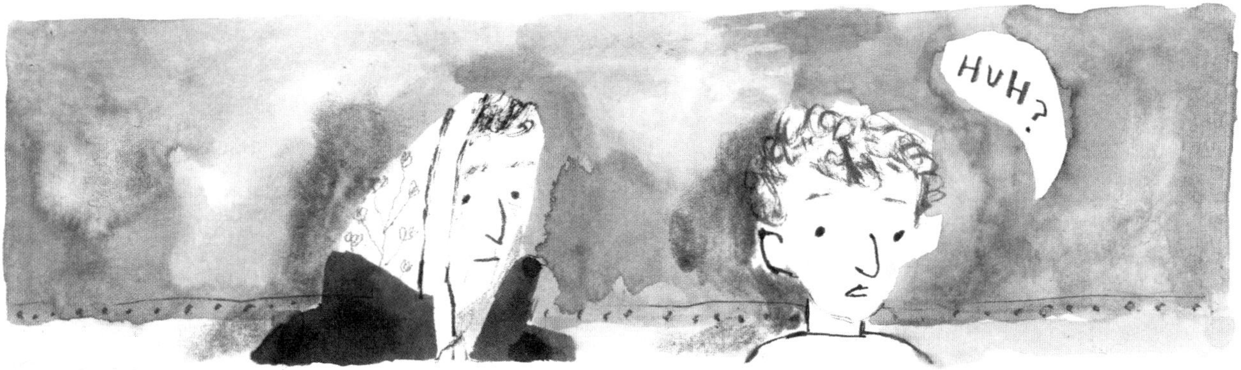
HUH?

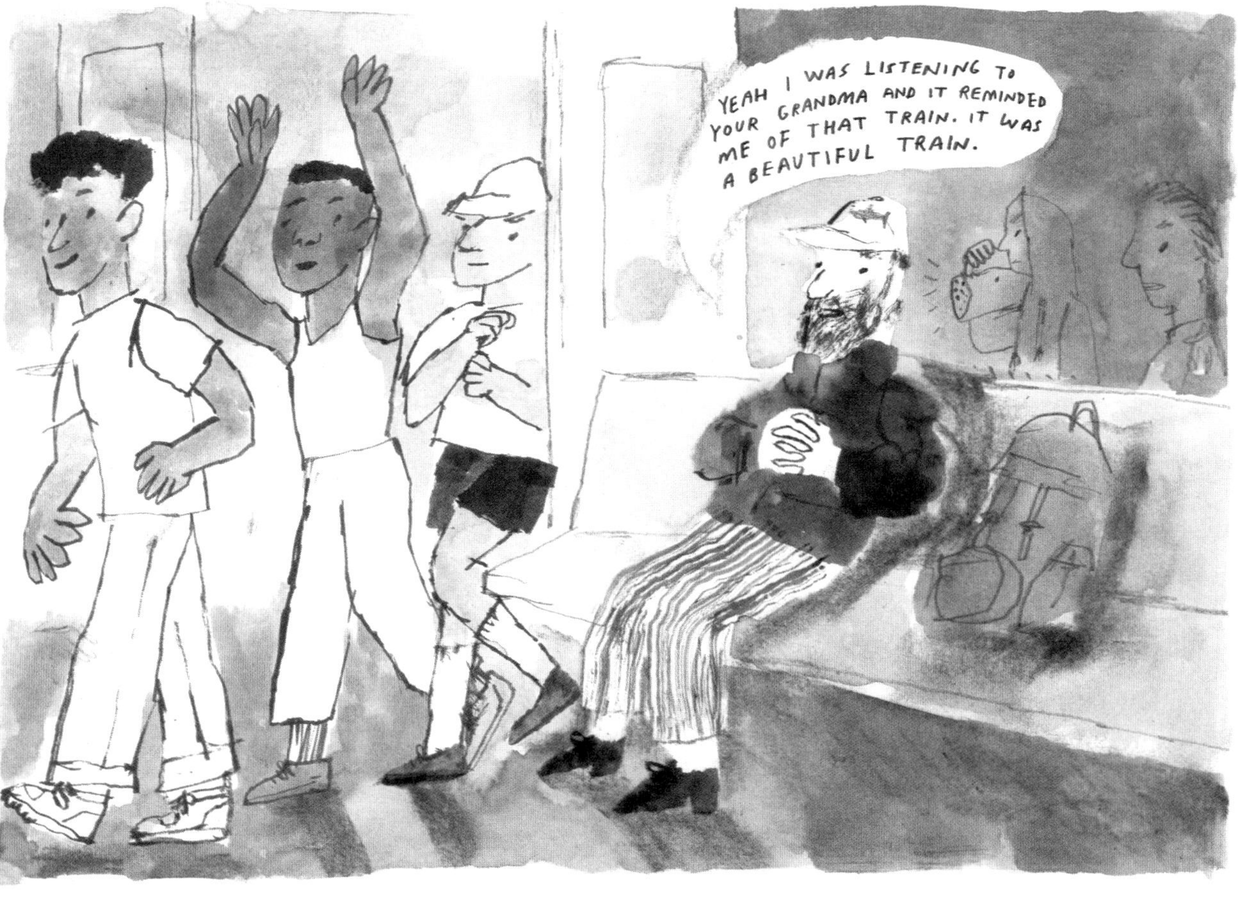
YEAH I WAS LISTENING TO YOUR GRANDMA AND IT REMINDED ME OF THAT TRAIN. IT WAS A BEAUTIFUL TRAIN.

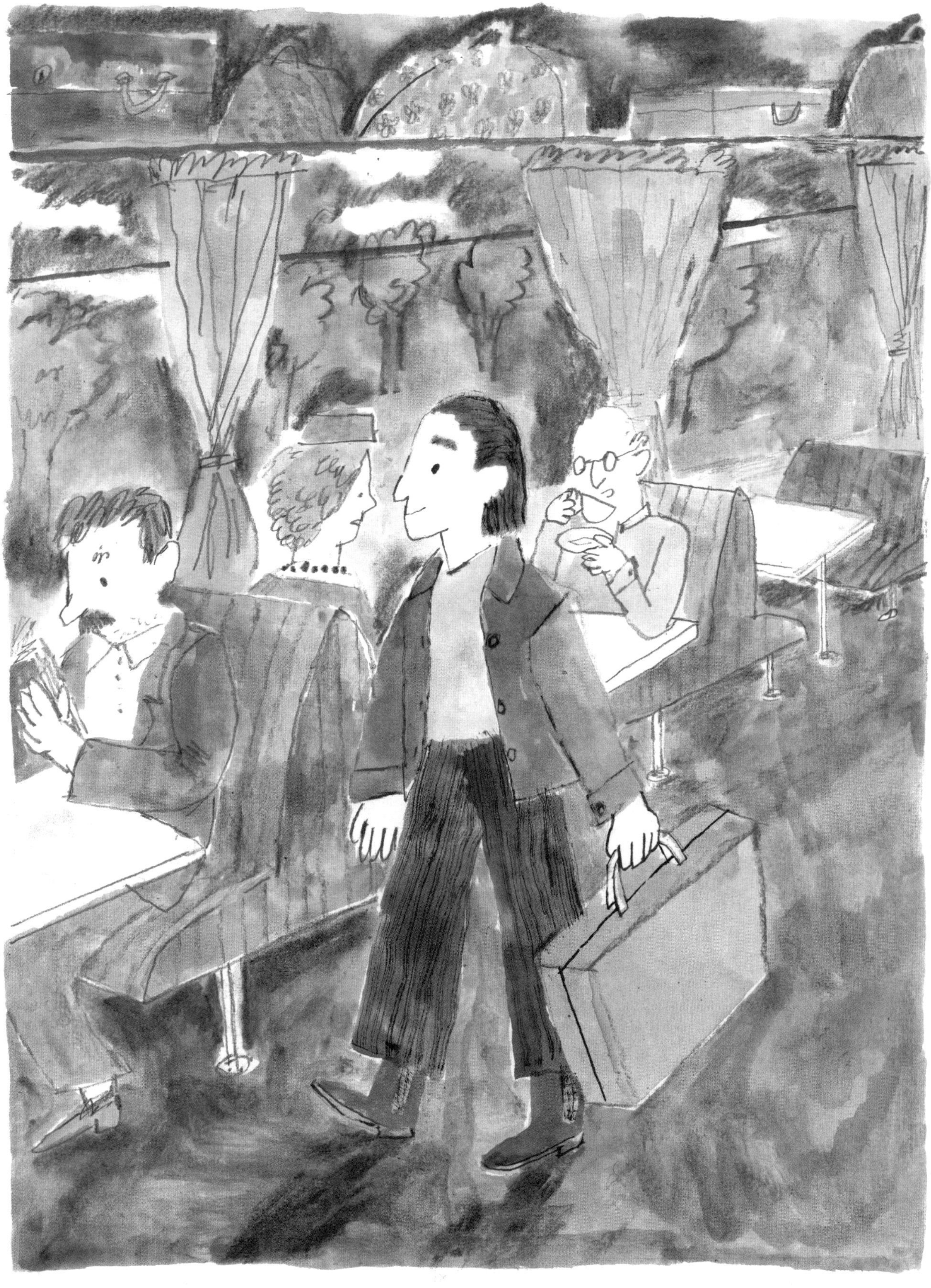

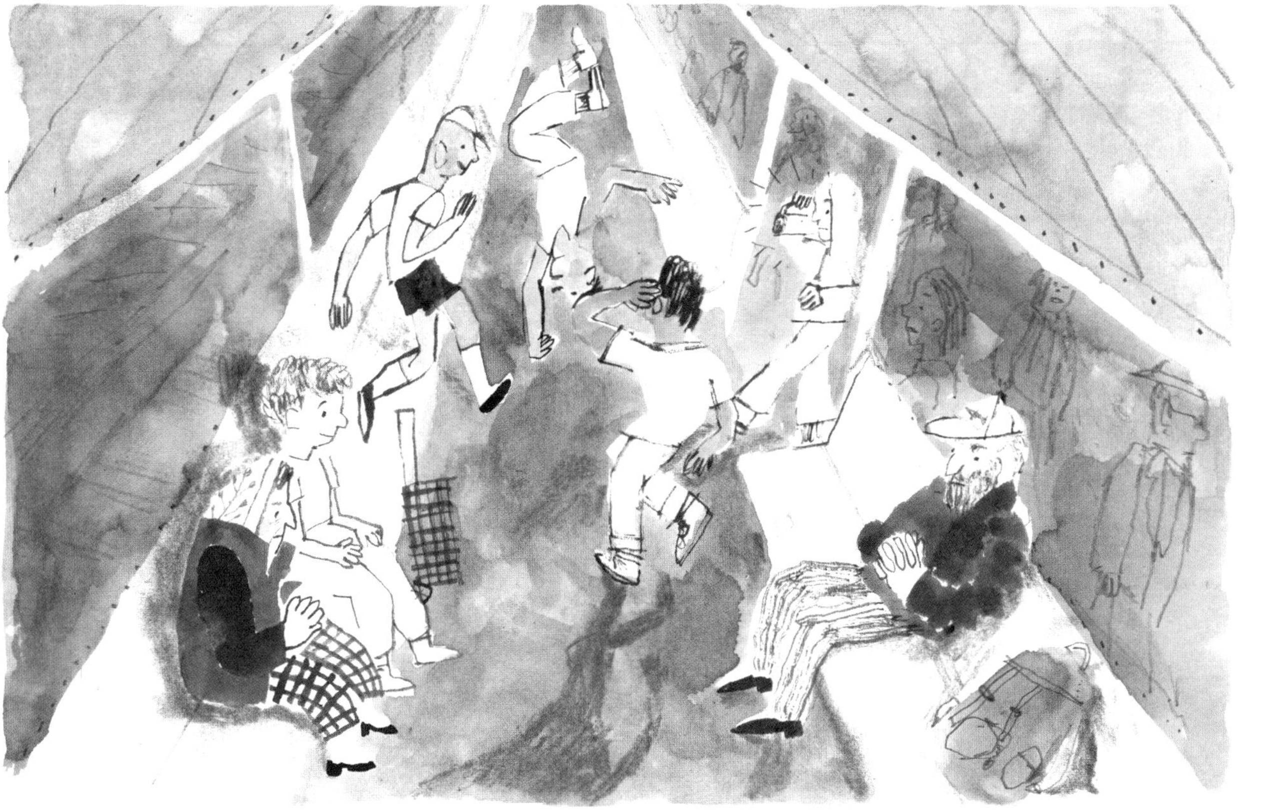

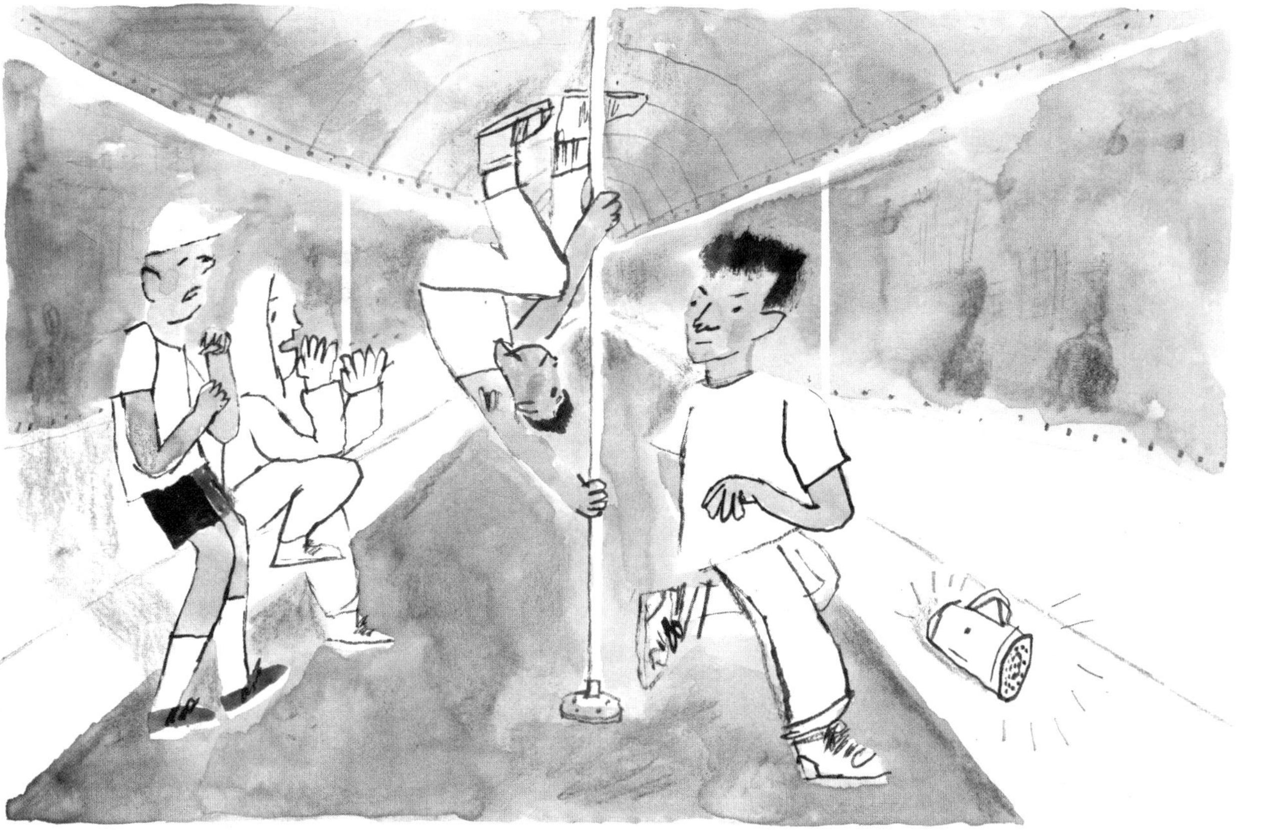

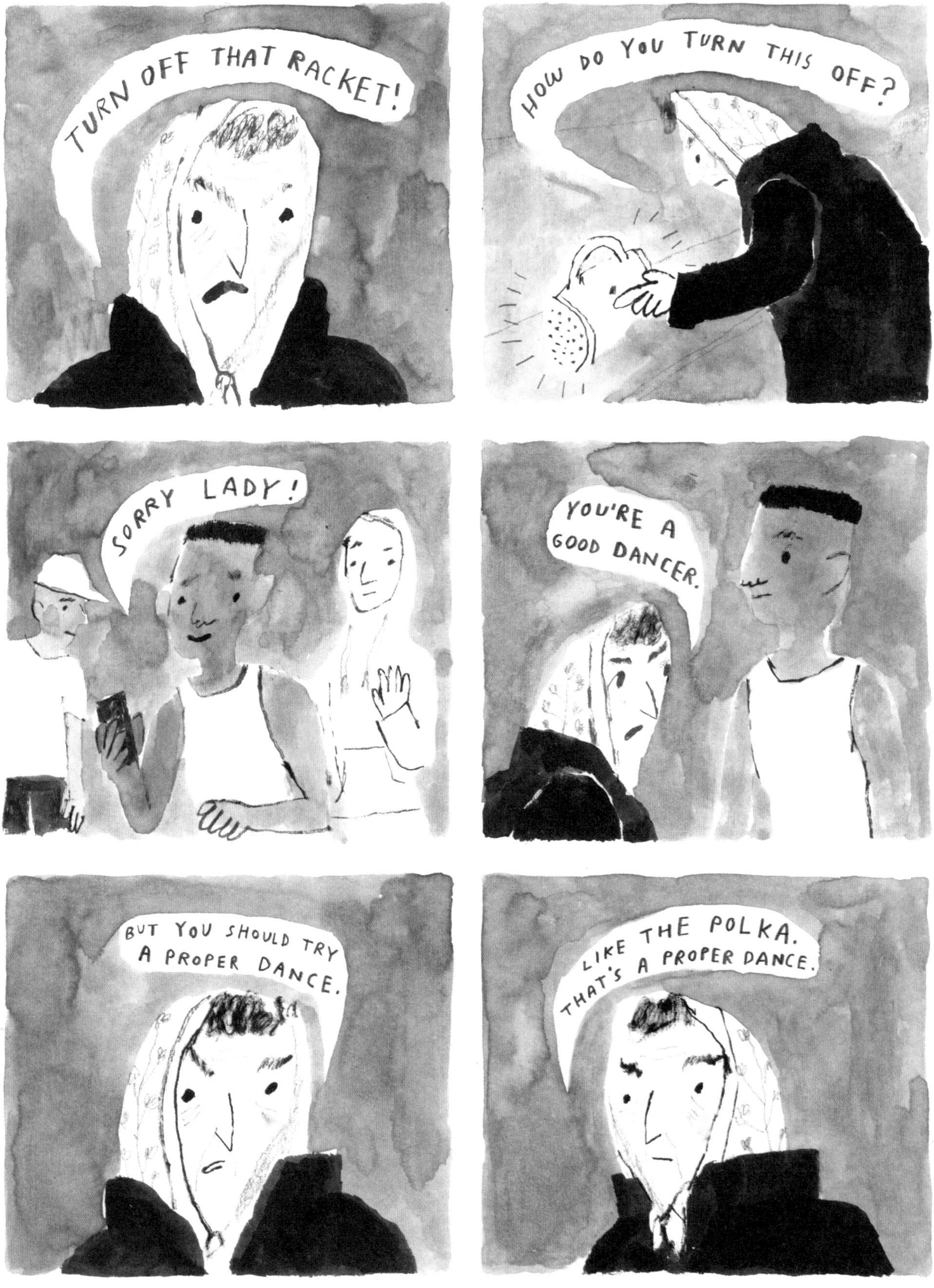
TURN OFF THAT RACKET!
HOW DO YOU TURN THIS OFF?
SORRY LADY!
YOU'RE A GOOD DANCER.
BUT YOU SHOULD TRY A PROPER DANCE.
LIKE THE POLKA. THAT'S A PROPER DANCE.

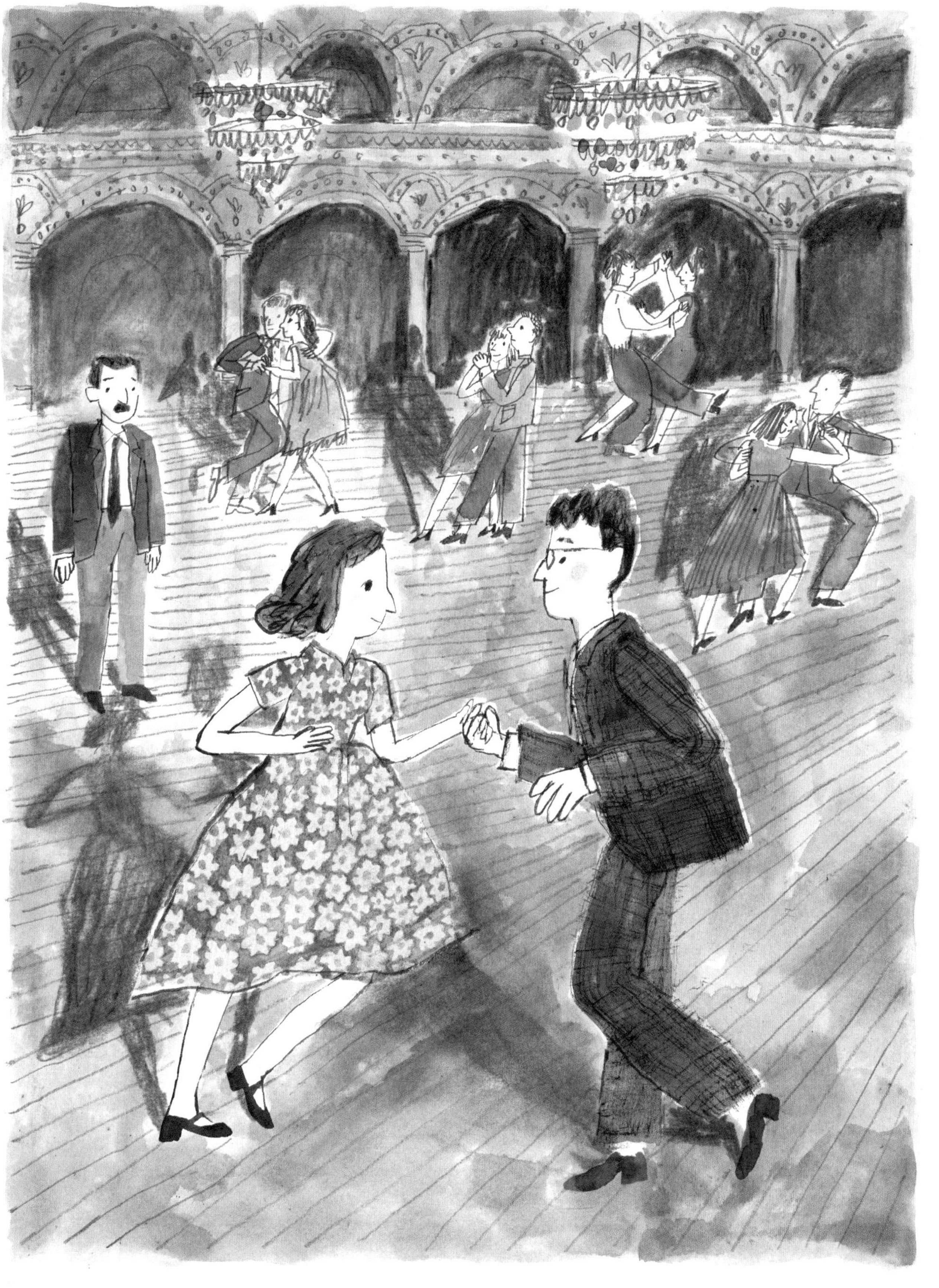

86TH STREET
WHERE AM I?
STOOGE
FLOWERS
YOU WANTED TO GO TO THE UPPER WEST SIDE, BUBBE.
THIS ISN'T THE UPPER WEST, BENJI.
OY, THEY GOT THE TRAIN WRONG.
WHERE IS GROSSINGERS?
WHERE IS RUSKAYS?
I DON'T KNOW BUBBE. IT'S ALL CHANGED.
EVERYTHING ALWAYS CHANGES. NOT JUST THE BAD THINGS BUT THE GOOD THINGS TOO.
BAYSPICE
WHY CHANGE SOMETHING THAT'S PERFECTLY GOOD? IT'S SO WASTEFUL.
nails
COME ON BUBBE, LET'S FIND SOMEWHERE TO SIT DOWN.

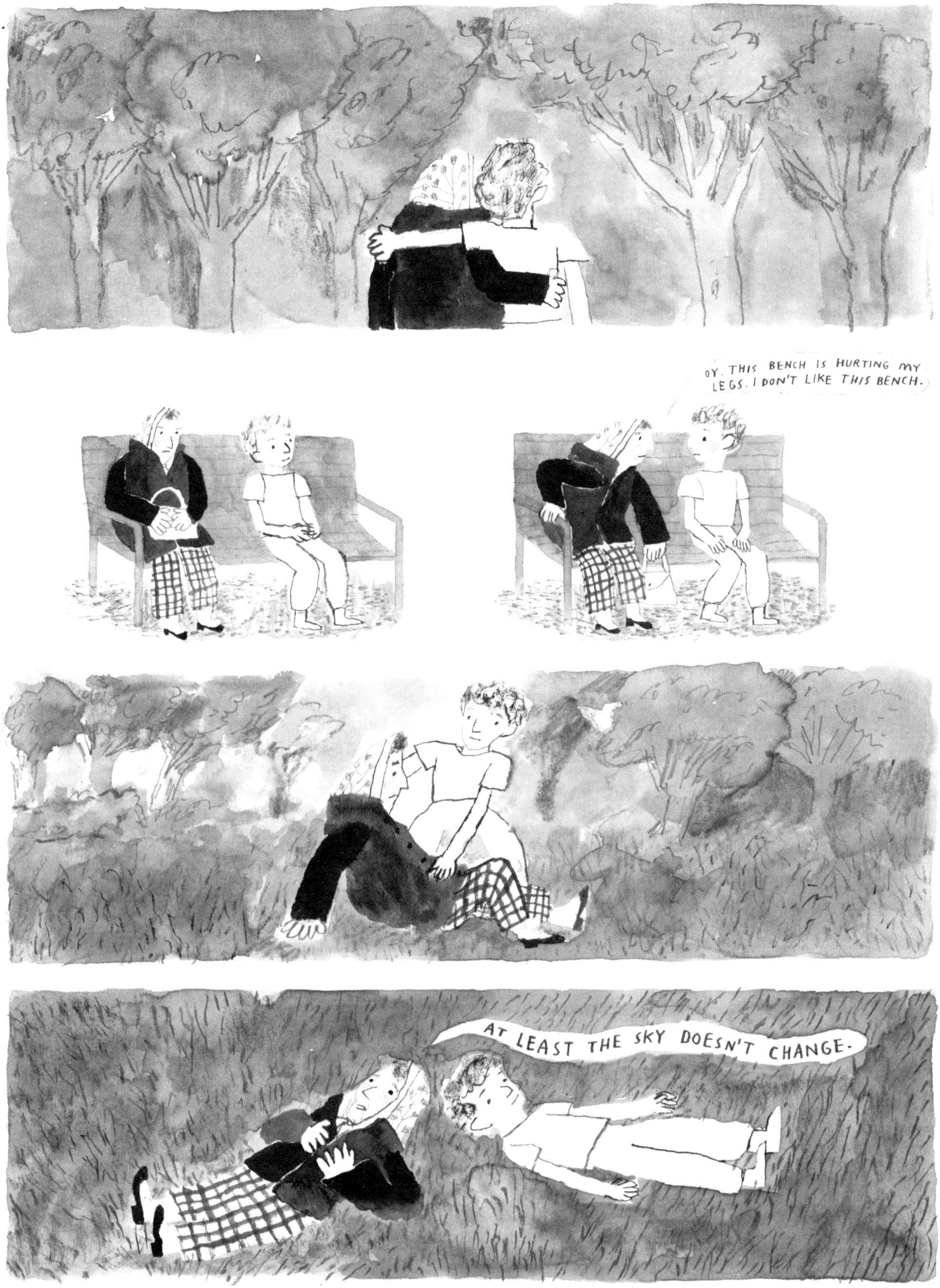
OY. THIS BENCH IS HURTING MY LEGS. I DON'T LIKE THIS BENCH.
AT LEAST THE SKY DOESN'T CHANGE.

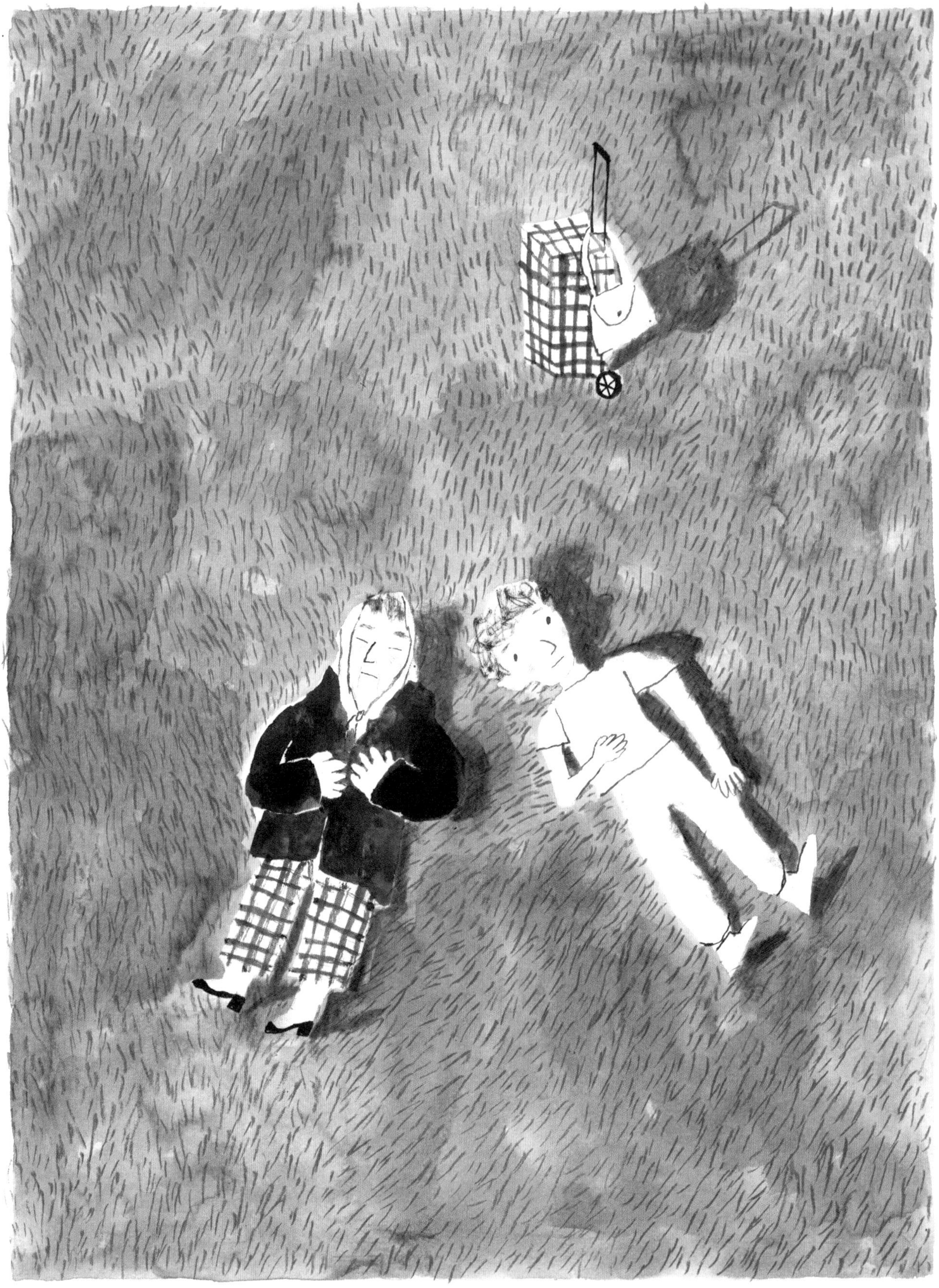

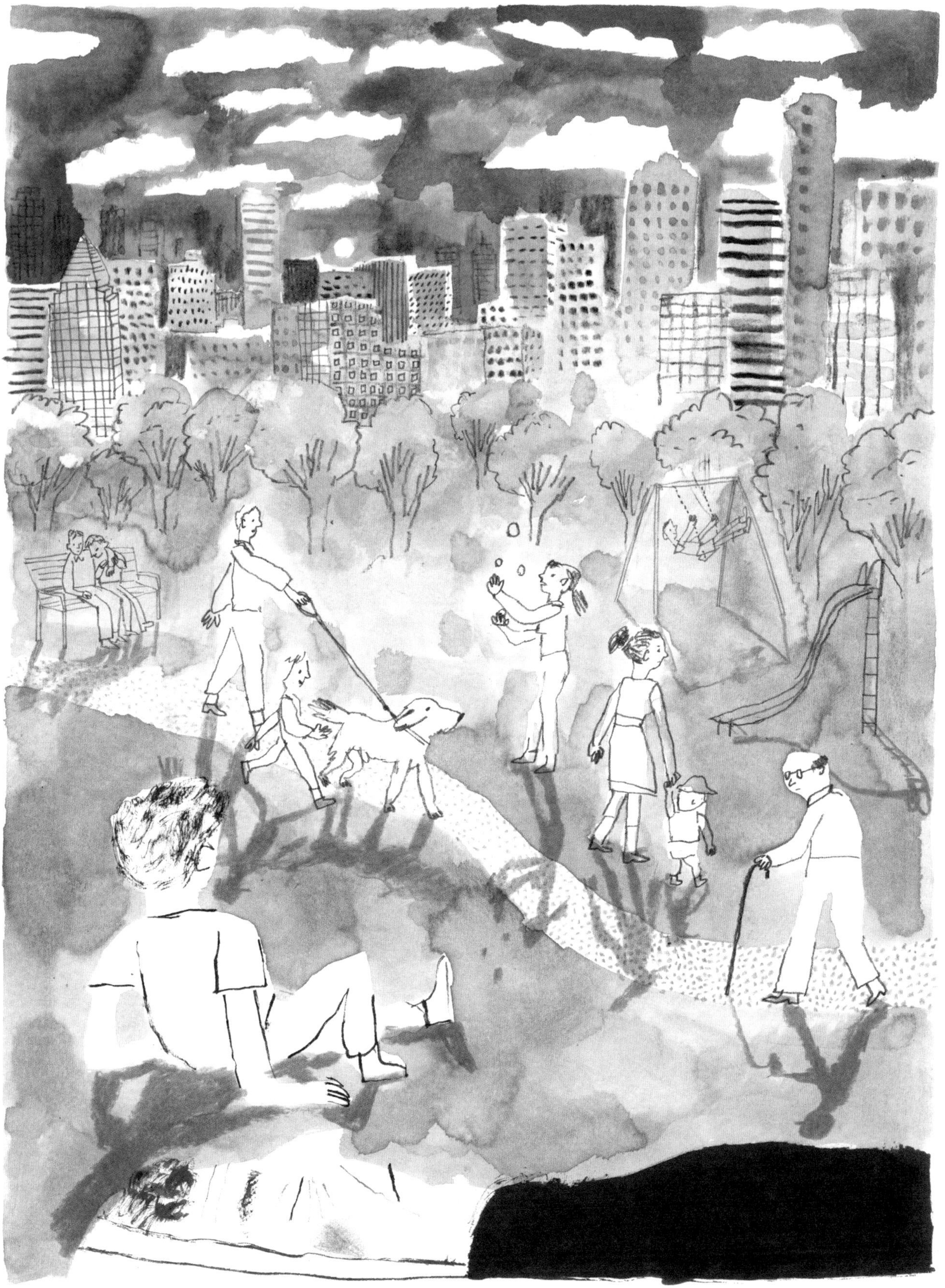

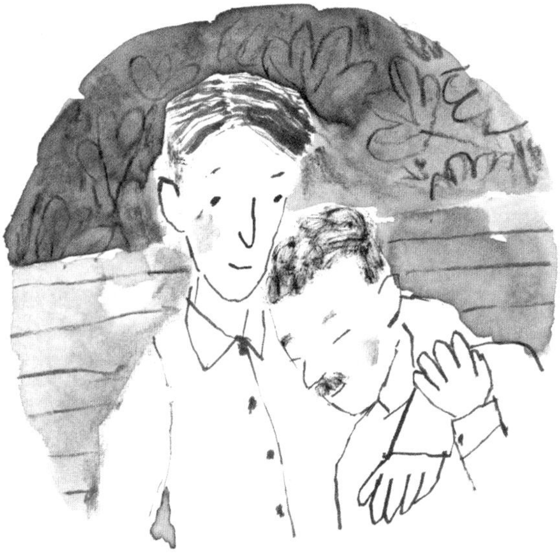

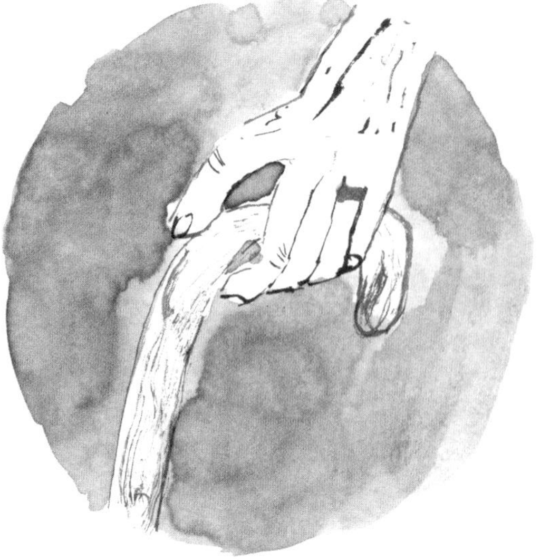

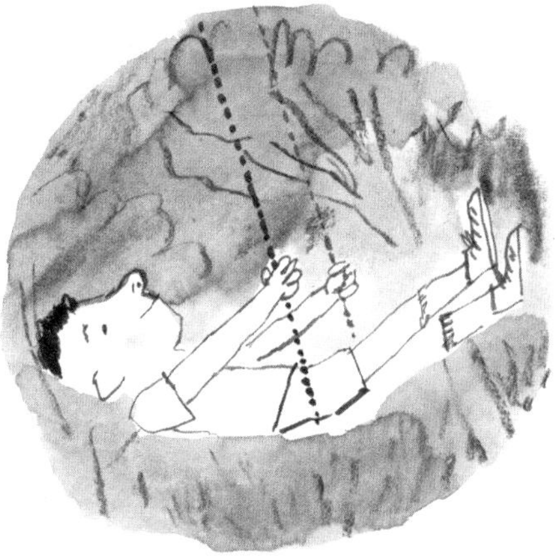

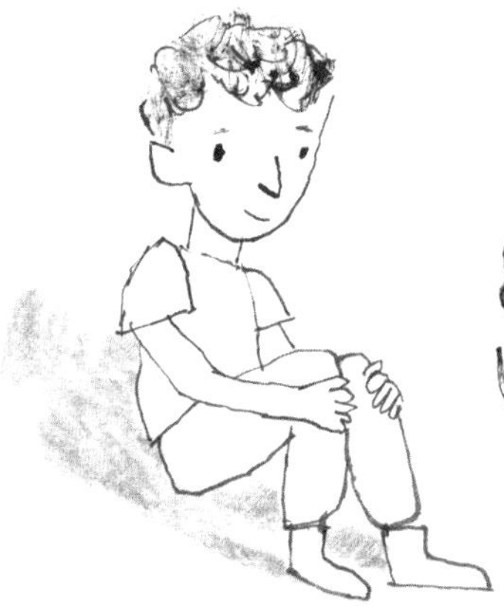

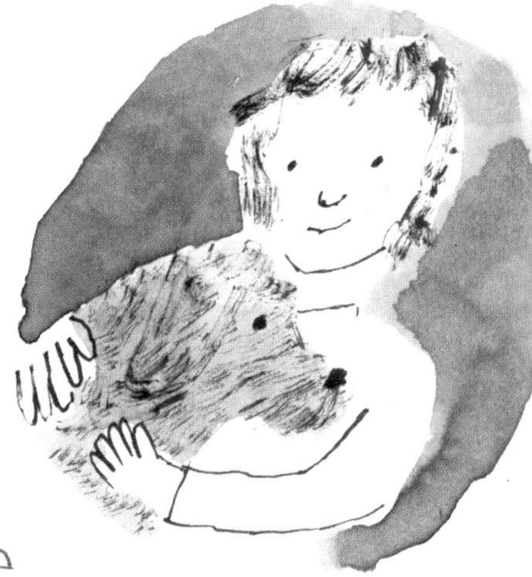

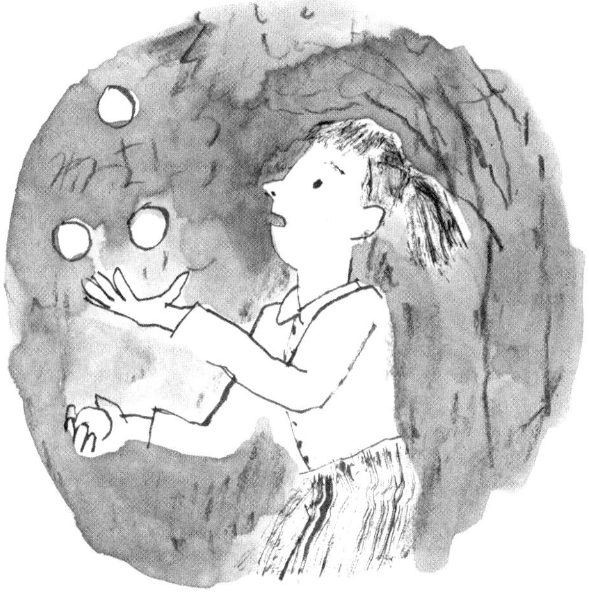

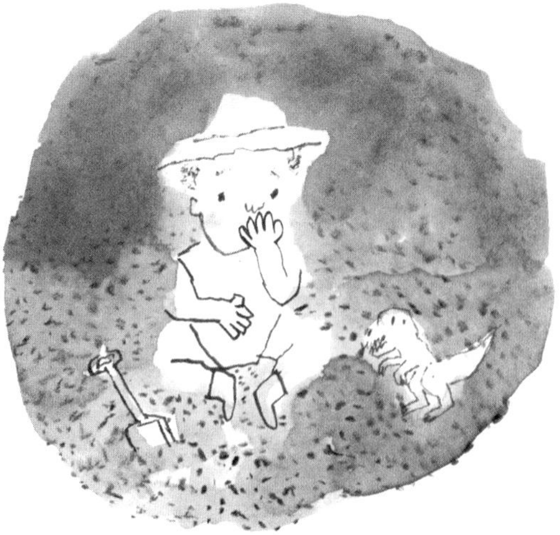

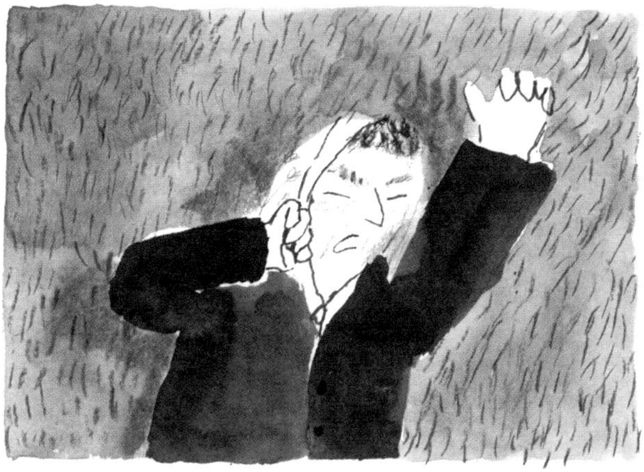

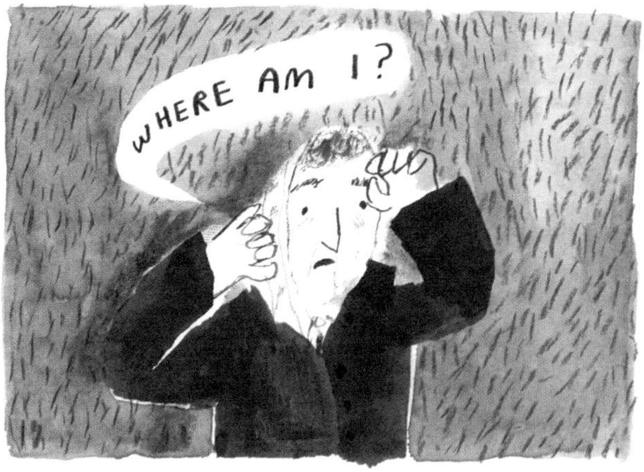
WHERE AM I?

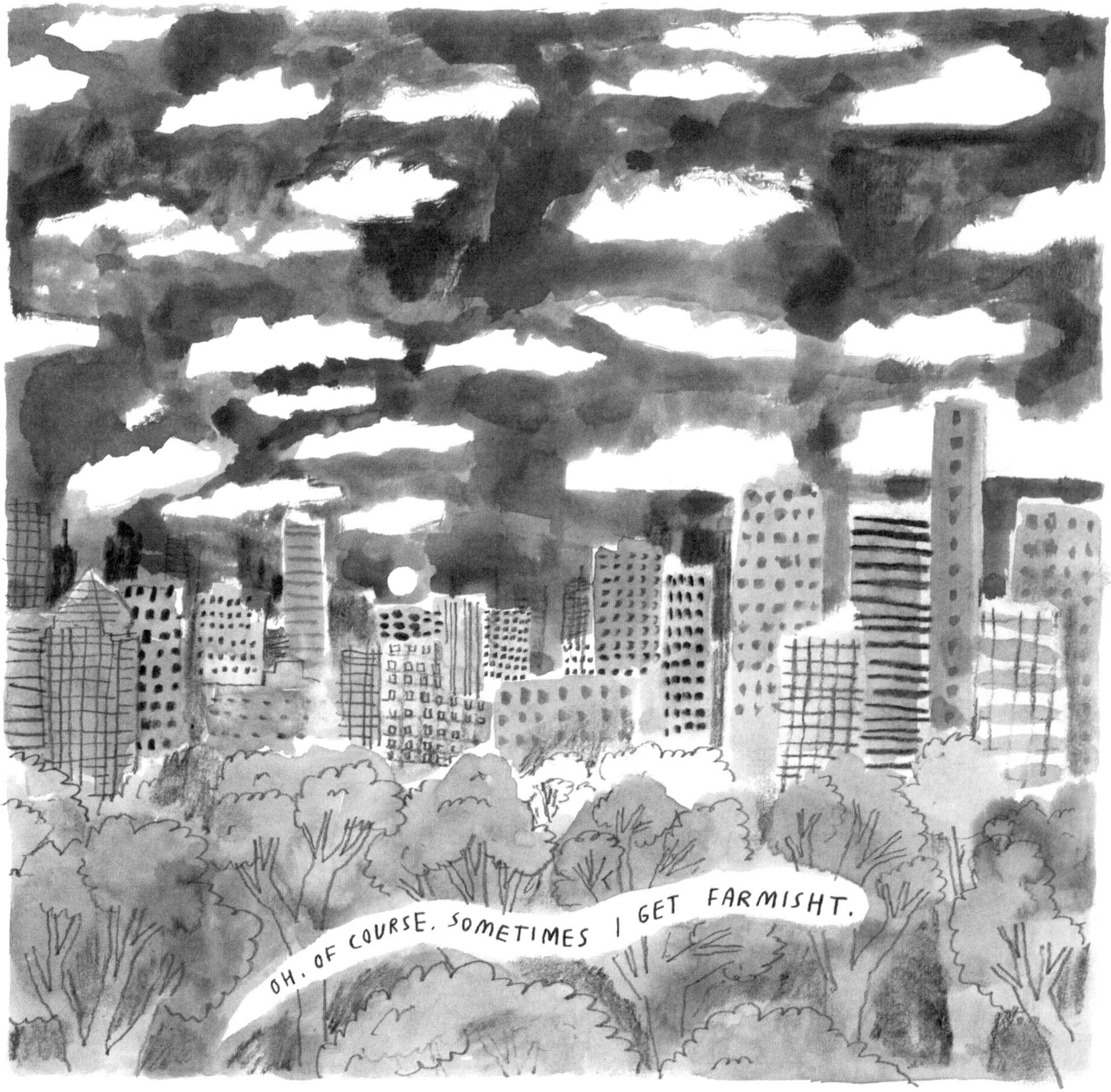
OH. OF COURSE. SOMETIMES I GET FARMISHT.

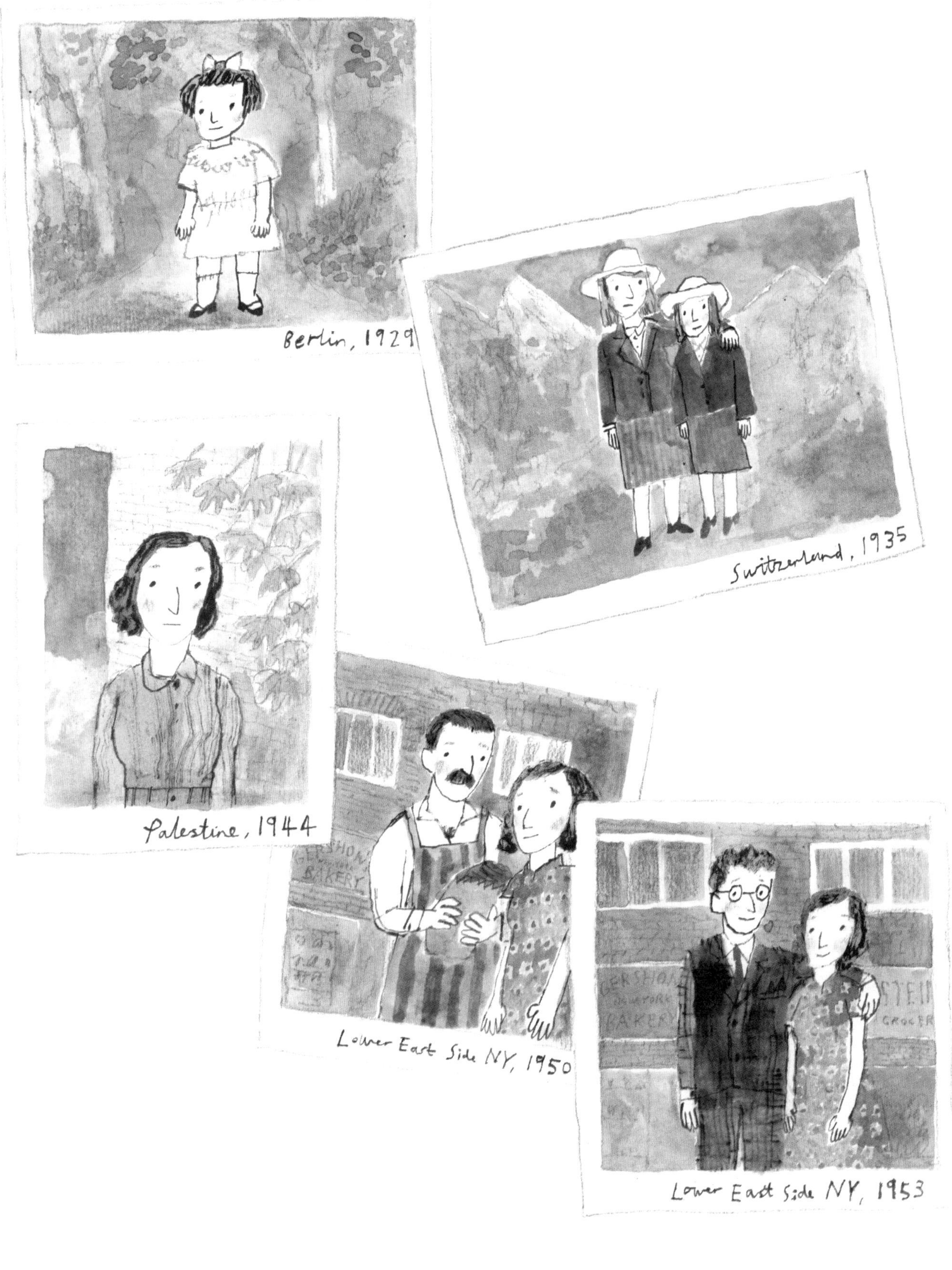
Berlin, 1929
Switzerland, 1935
Palestine, 1944
Lower East Side NY, 1950
Lower East Side NY, 1953

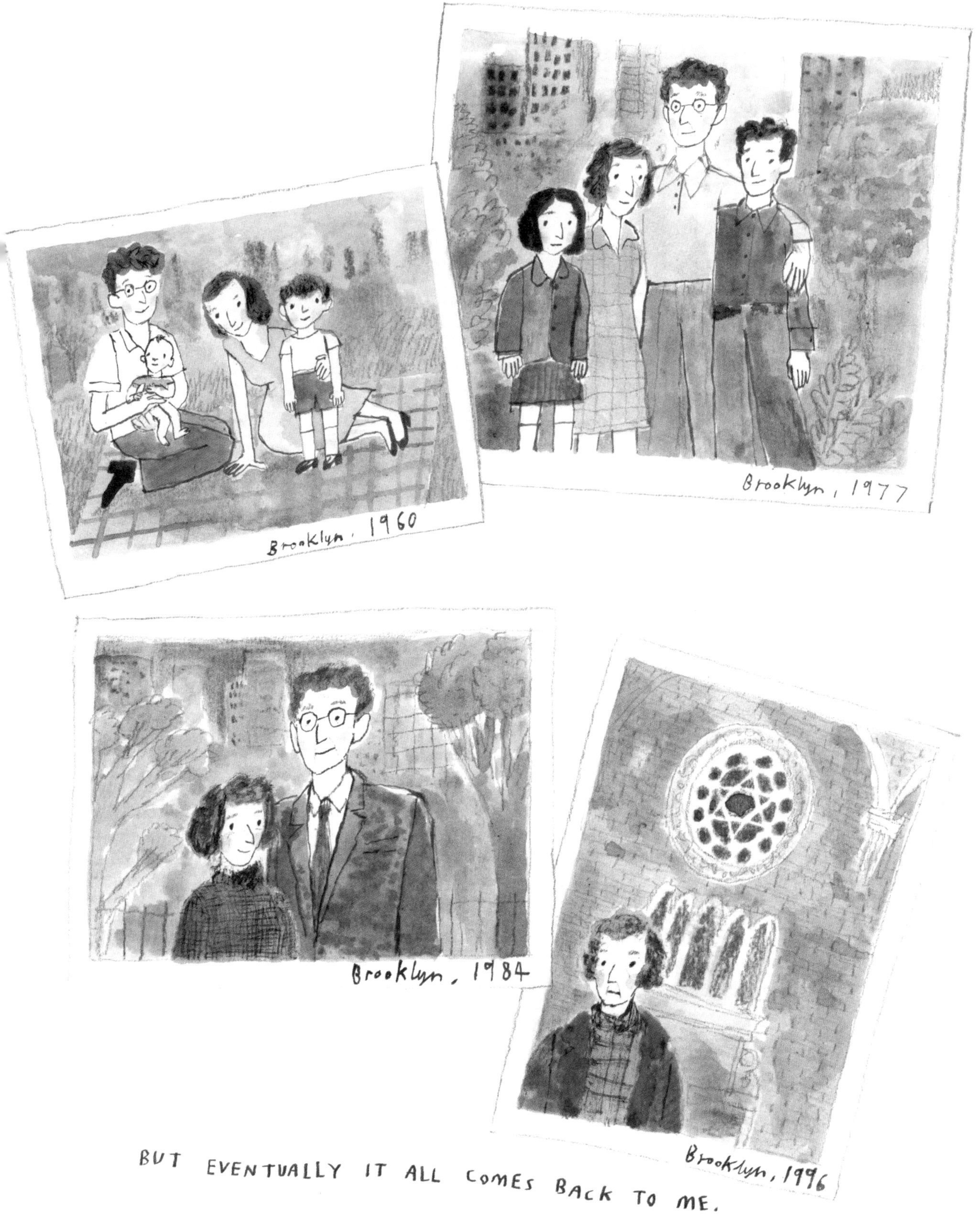
Brooklyn, 1960
Brooklyn, 1977
Brooklyn, 1984
Brooklyn, 1996
BUT EVENTUALLY IT ALL COMES BACK TO ME.

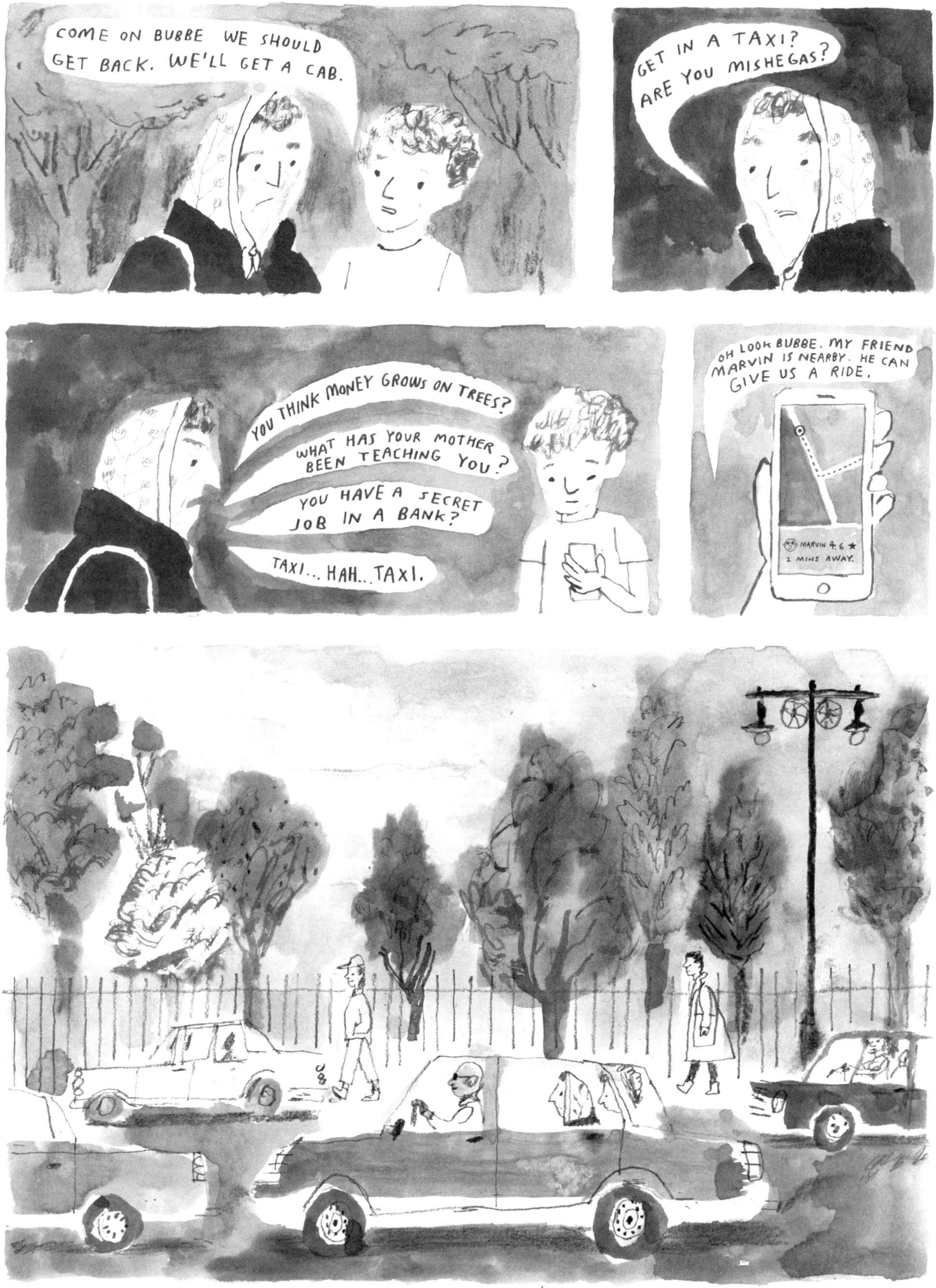
COME ON BUBBE WE SHOULD GET BACK. WE'LL GET A CAB.
GET IN A TAXI? ARE YOU MISHEGAS?
YOU THINK MONEY GROWS ON TREES?
WHAT HAS YOUR MOTHER BEEN TEACHING YOU?
YOU HAVE A SECRET JOB IN A BANK?
TAXI... HAH... TAXI.
OH LOOK BUBBE. MY FRIEND MARVIN IS NEARBY. HE CAN GIVE US A RIDE.
MARVIN 4.6 ★
2 MINS AWAY.

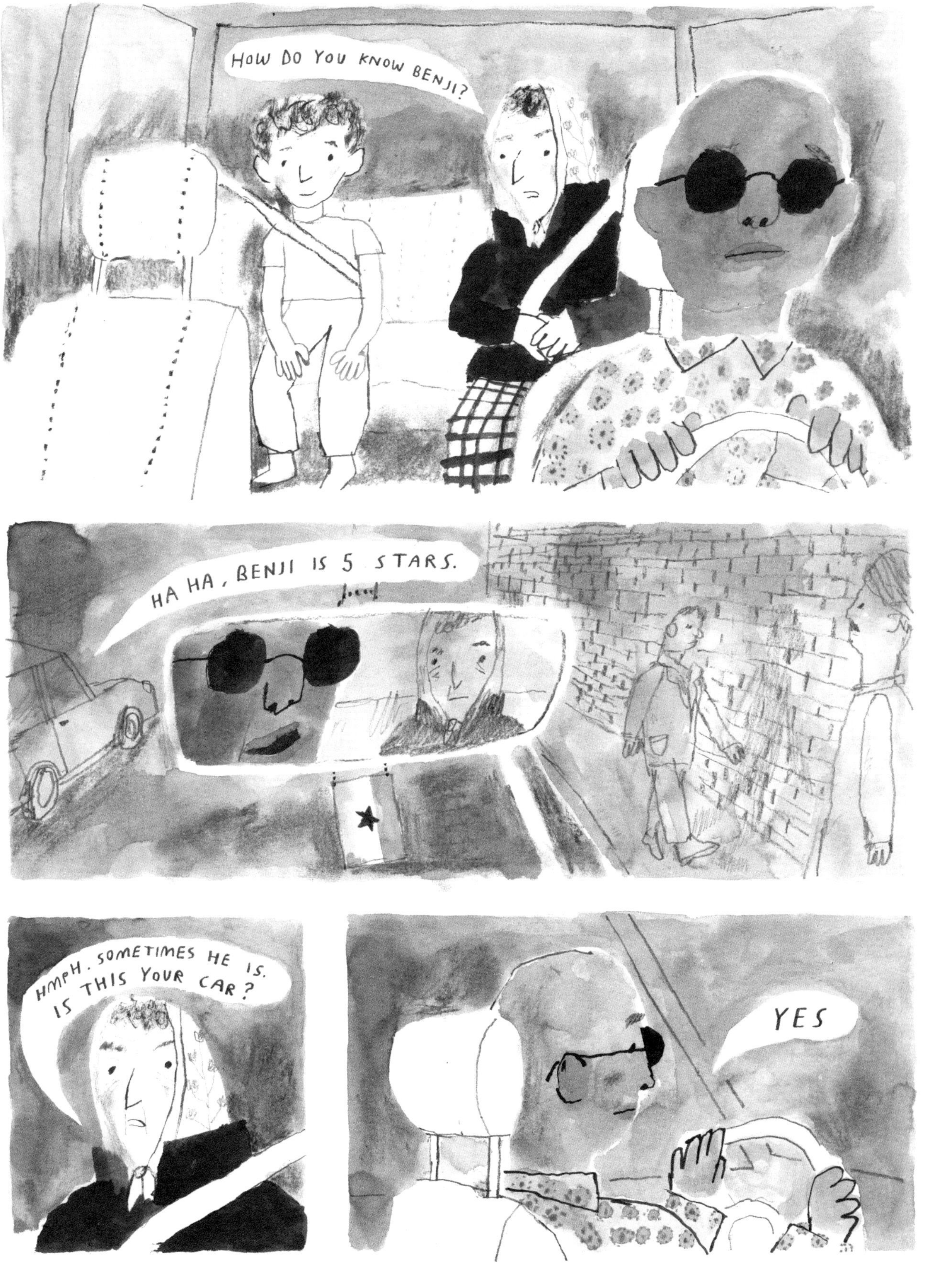
HOW DO YOU KNOW BENJI?
HA HA, BENJI IS 5 STARS.
HMPH. SOMETIMES HE IS. IS THIS YOUR CAR?
YES

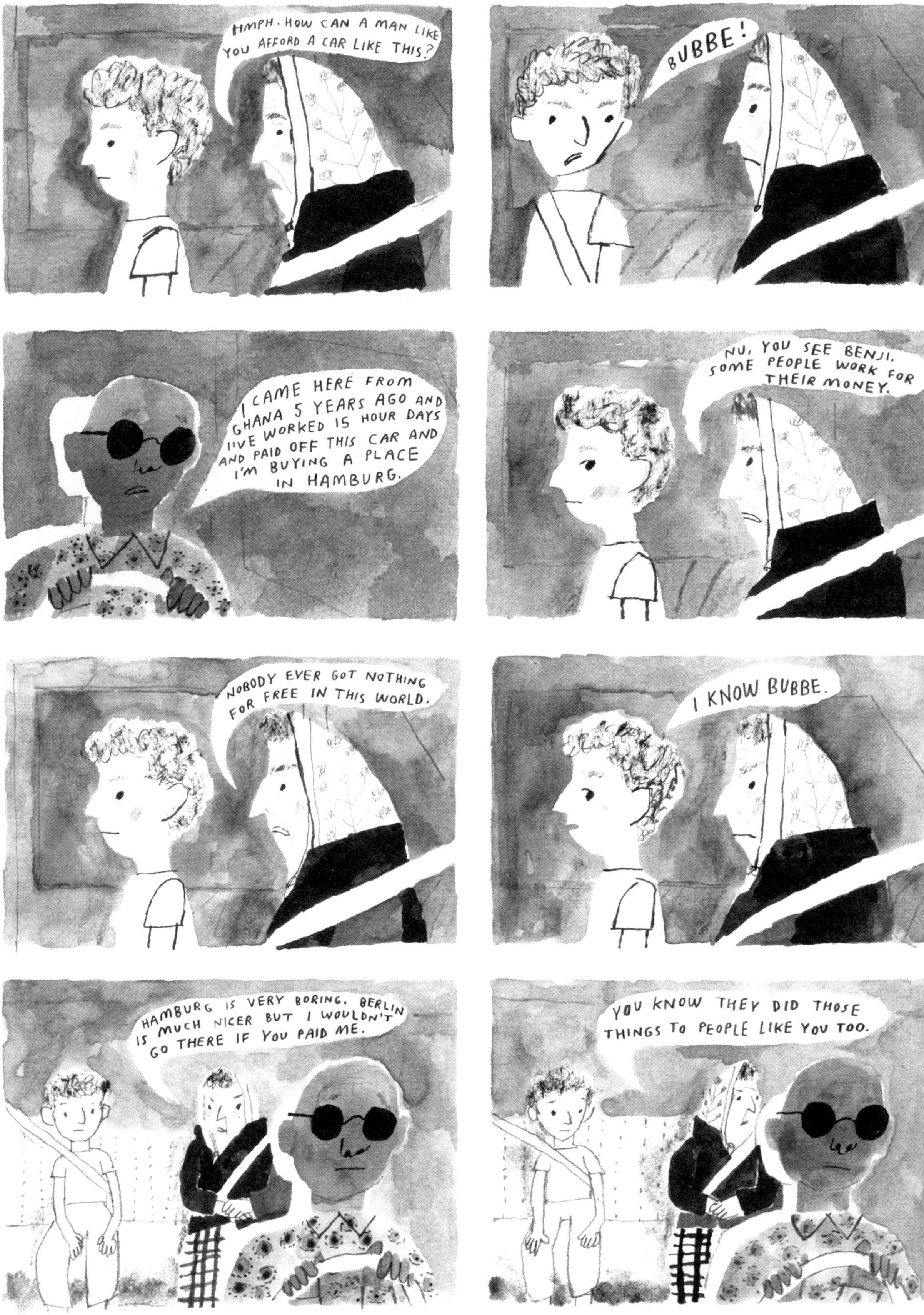
HMPH. HOW CAN A MAN LIKE YOU AFFORD A CAR LIKE THIS?
BUBBE!
I CAME HERE FROM GHANA 5 YEARS AGO AND I'VE WORKED 15 HOUR DAYS AND PAID OFF THIS CAR AND I'M BUYING A PLACE IN HAMBURG.
NU, YOU SEE BENJI. SOME PEOPLE WORK FOR THEIR MONEY.
NOBODY EVER GOT NOTHING FOR FREE IN THIS WORLD.
I KNOW BUBBE.
HAMBURG IS VERY BORING. BERLIN IS MUCH NICER BUT I WOULDN'T GO THERE IF YOU PAID ME.
YOU KNOW THEY DID THOSE THINGS TO PEOPLE LIKE YOU TOO.

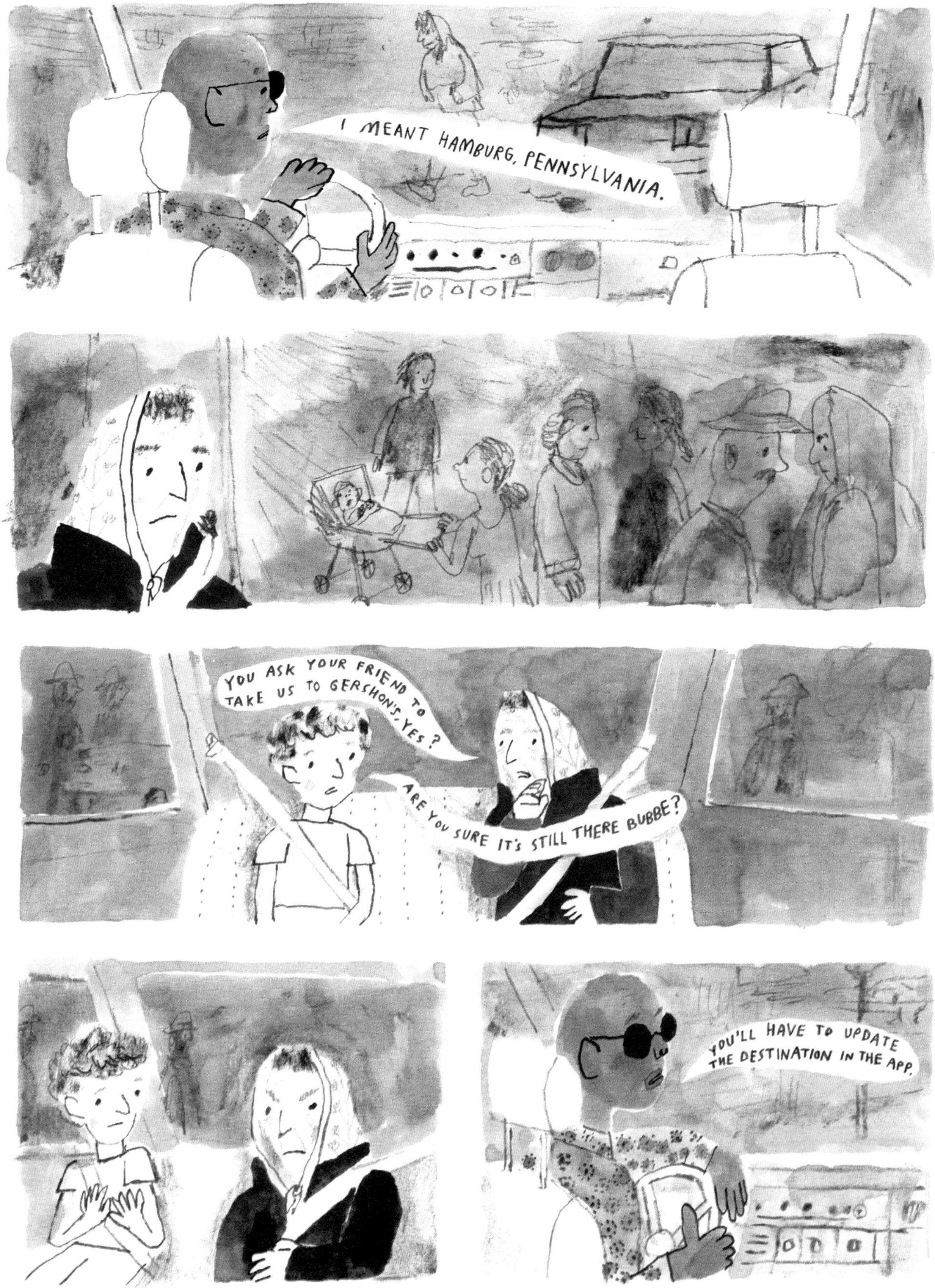
I MEANT HAMBURG, PENNSYLVANIA.
YOU ASK YOUR FRIEND TO TAKE US TO GERSHON'S, YES?
ARE YOU SURE IT'S STILL THERE BUBBE?
YOU'LL HAVE TO UPDATE THE DESTINATION IN THE APP.

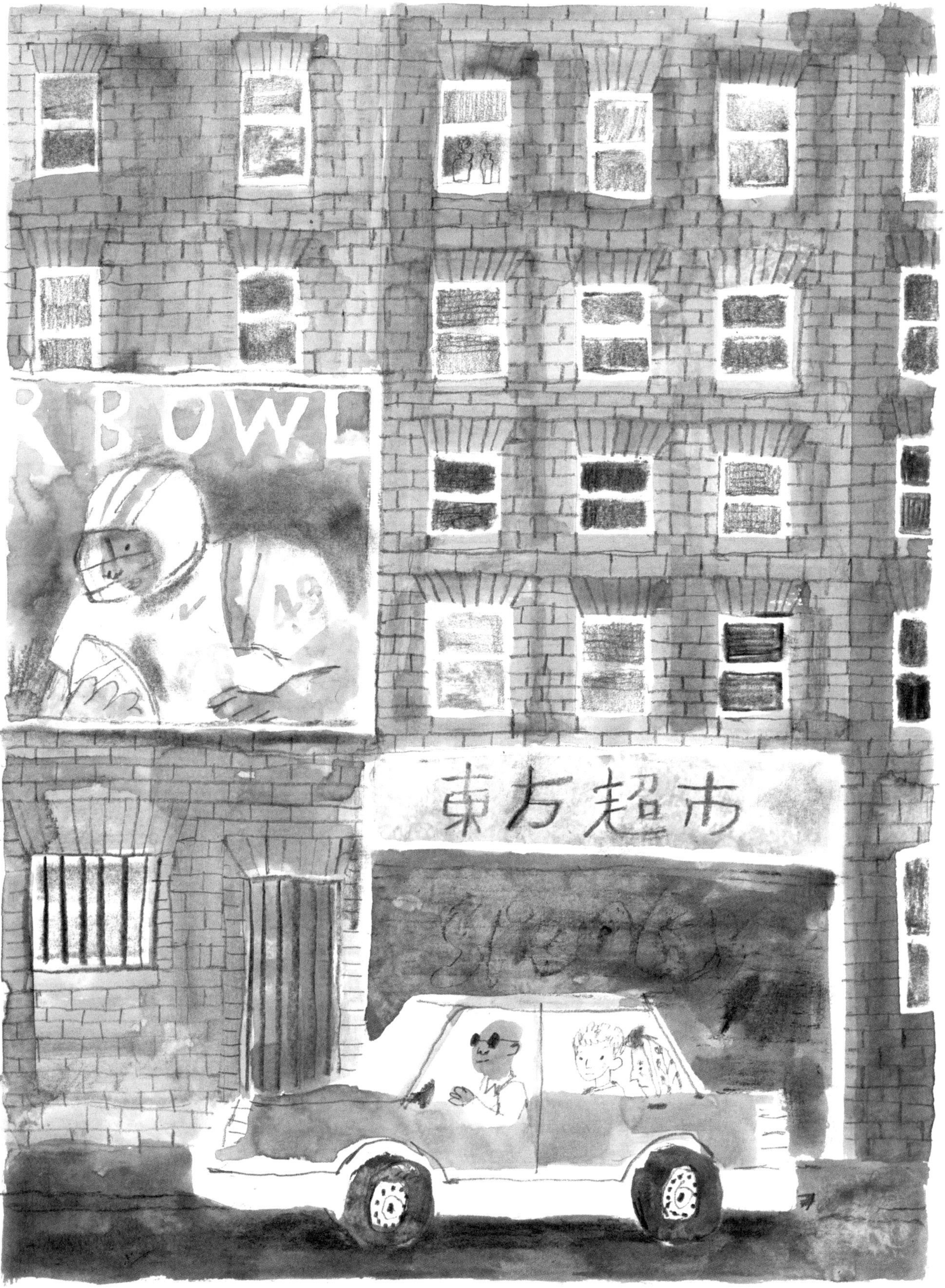
R BOWL
東方超市

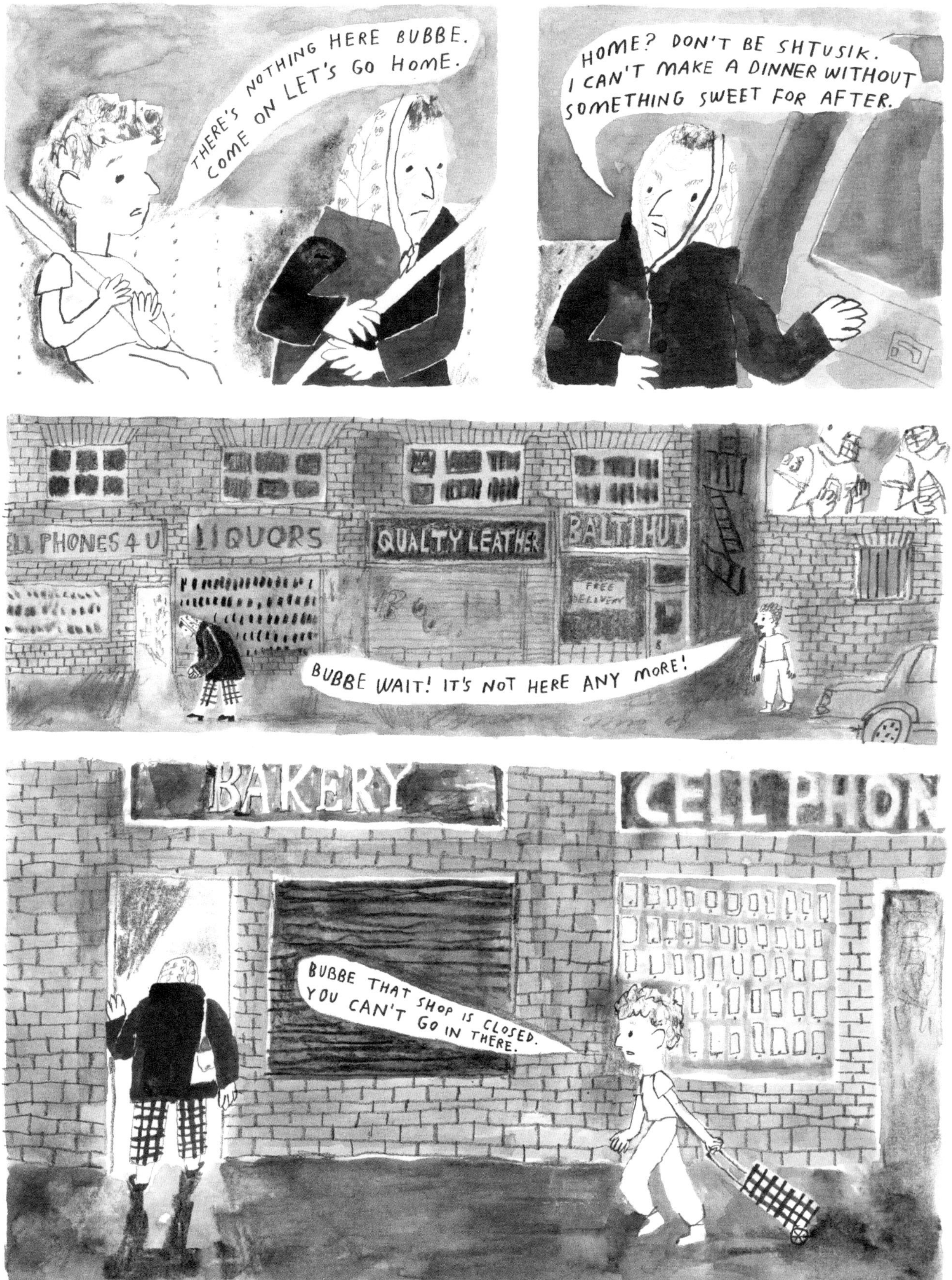
THERE'S NOTHING HERE BUBBE. COME ON LET'S GO HOME.
HOME? DON'T BE SHTUSIK. I CAN'T MAKE A DINNER WITHOUT SOMETHING SWEET FOR AFTER.
ELL PHONES 4 U
LIQUORS
QUALTY LEATHER
BALTI HUT
FREE DELIVERY
BUBBE WAIT! IT'S NOT HERE ANY MORE!
BAKERY
CELL PHON
BUBBE THAT SHOP IS CLOSED. YOU CAN'T GO IN THERE.

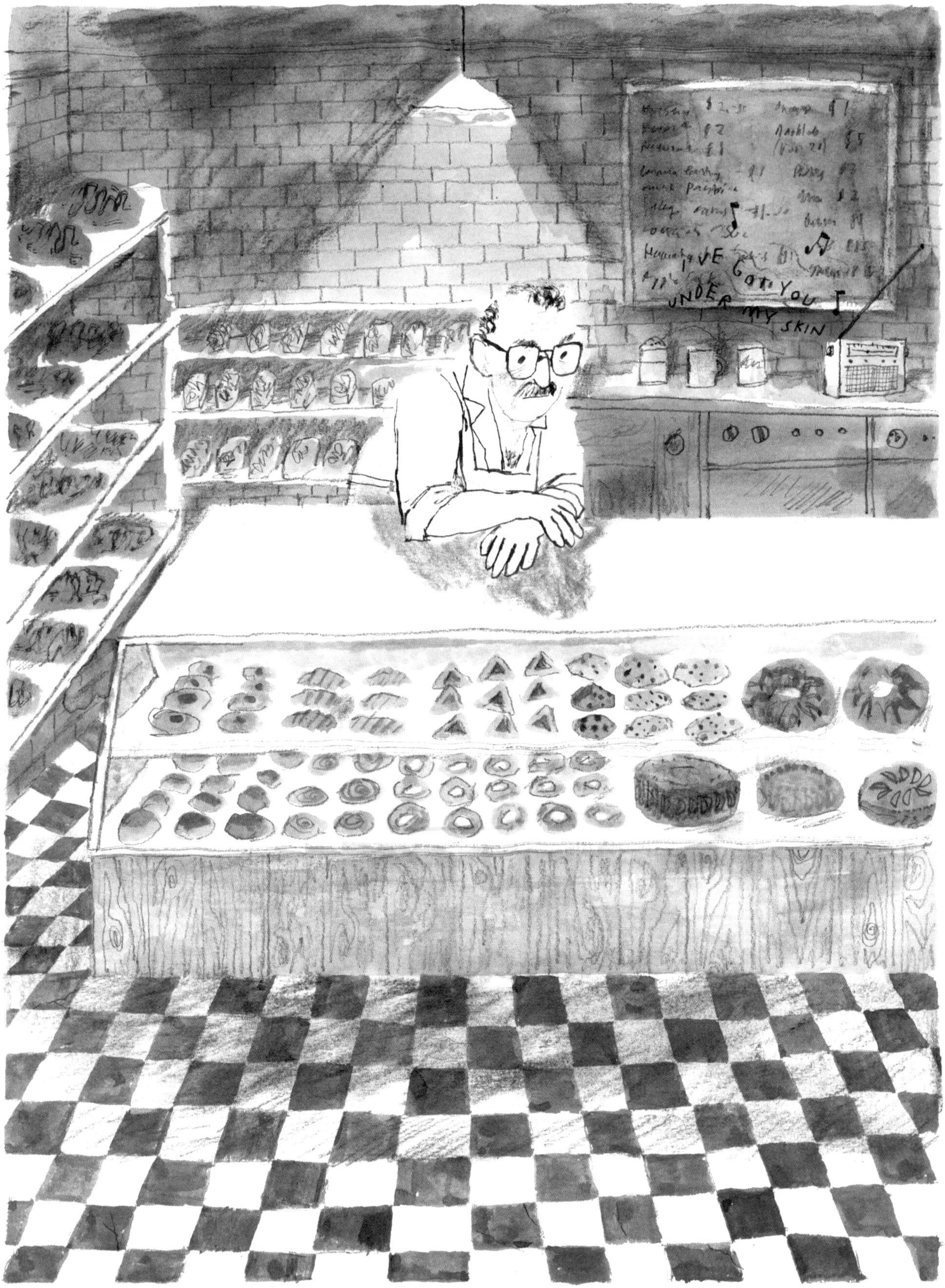
I'VE GOT YOU UNDER MY SKIN

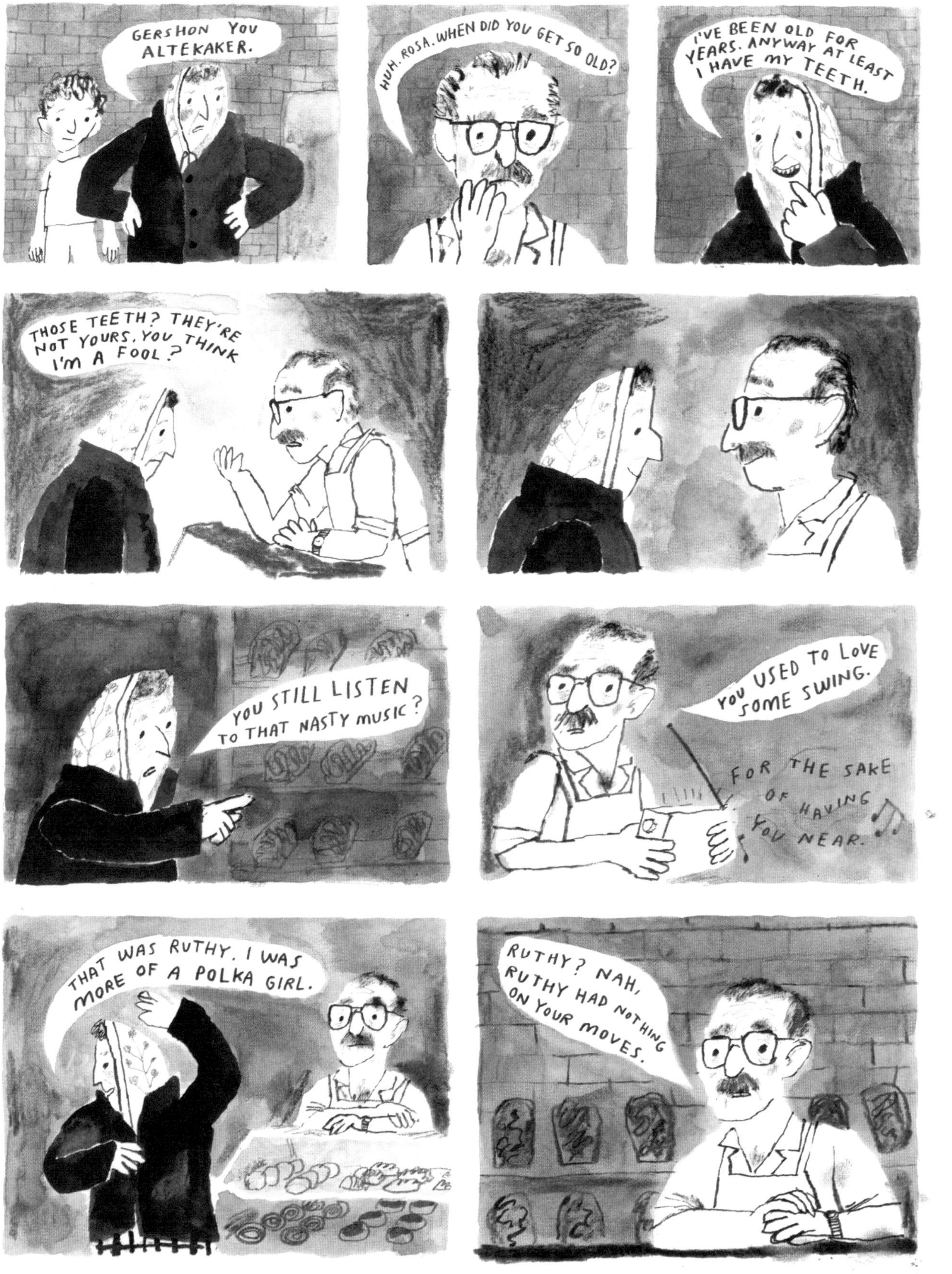
GERSHON YOU ALTEKAKER.
HUH, ROSA. WHEN DID YOU GET SO OLD?
I'VE BEEN OLD FOR YEARS. ANYWAY AT LEAST I HAVE MY TEETH.
THOSE TEETH? THEY'RE NOT YOURS. YOU THINK I'M A FOOL?
YOU STILL LISTEN TO THAT NASTY MUSIC?
YOU USED TO LOVE SOME SWING.
FOR THE SAKE OF HAVING YOU NEAR.
THAT WAS RUTHY. I WAS MORE OF A POLKA GIRL.
RUTHY? NAH, RUTHY HAD NOTHING ON YOUR MOVES.

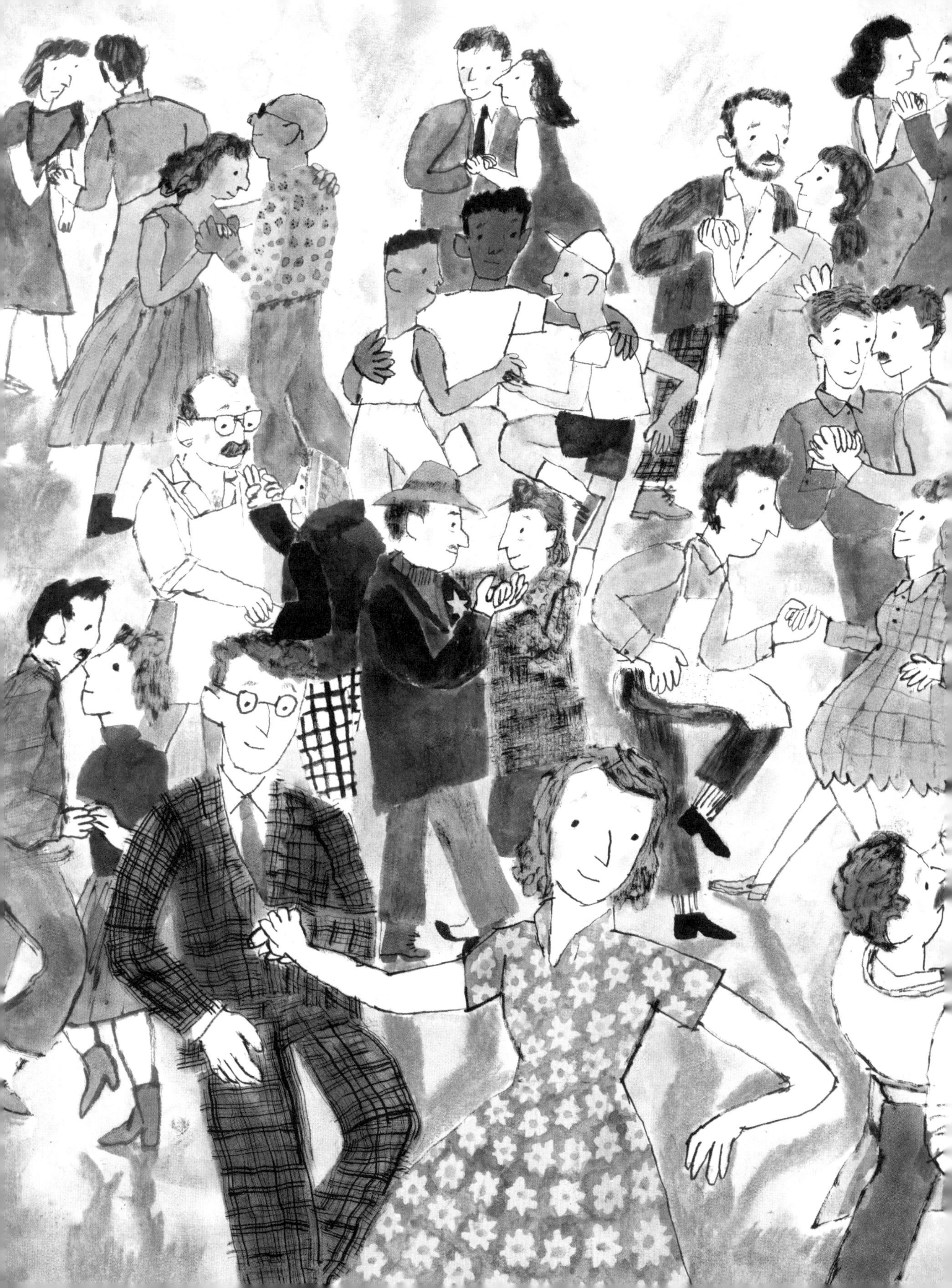

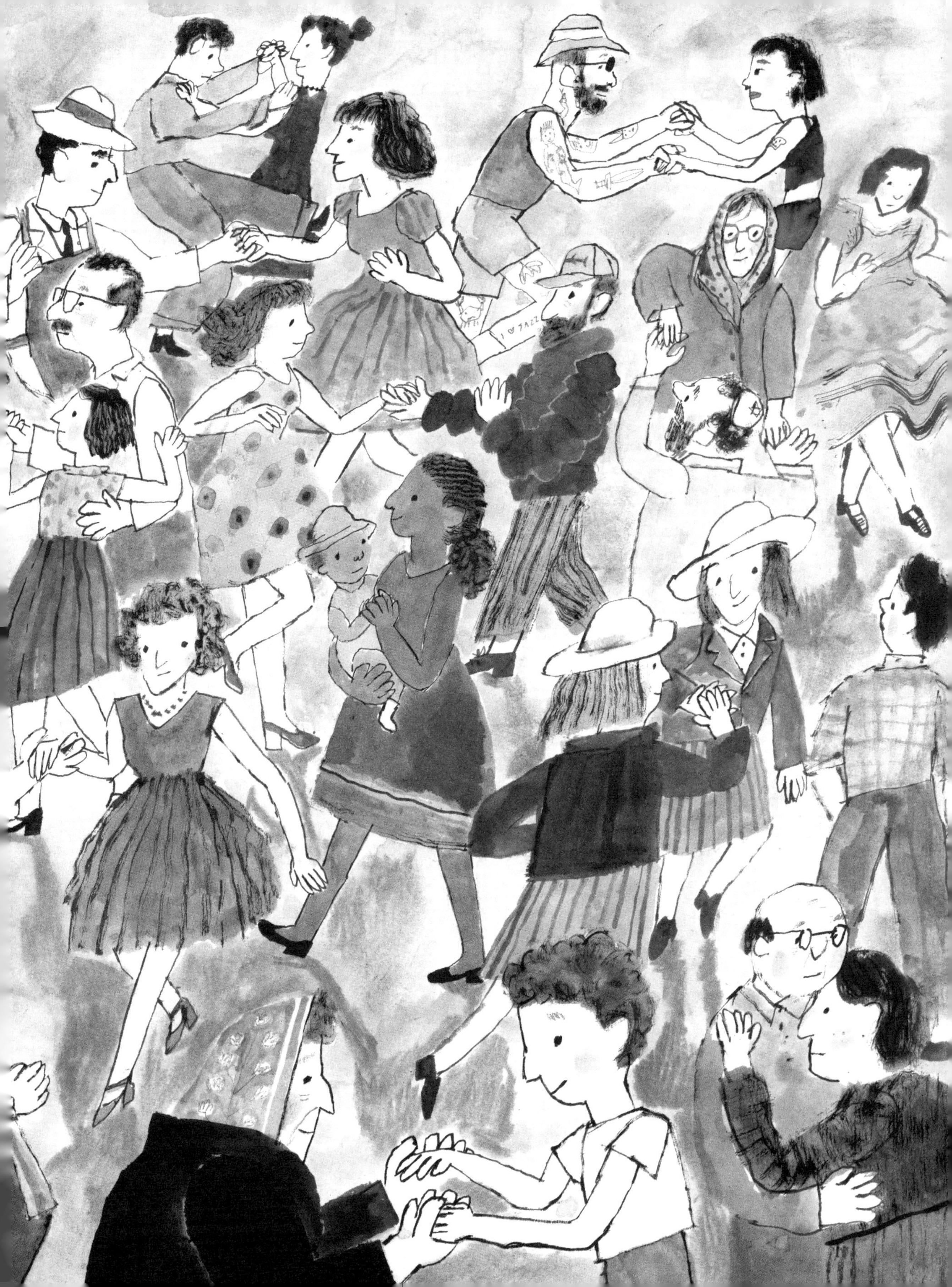
I ♥ JAZZ

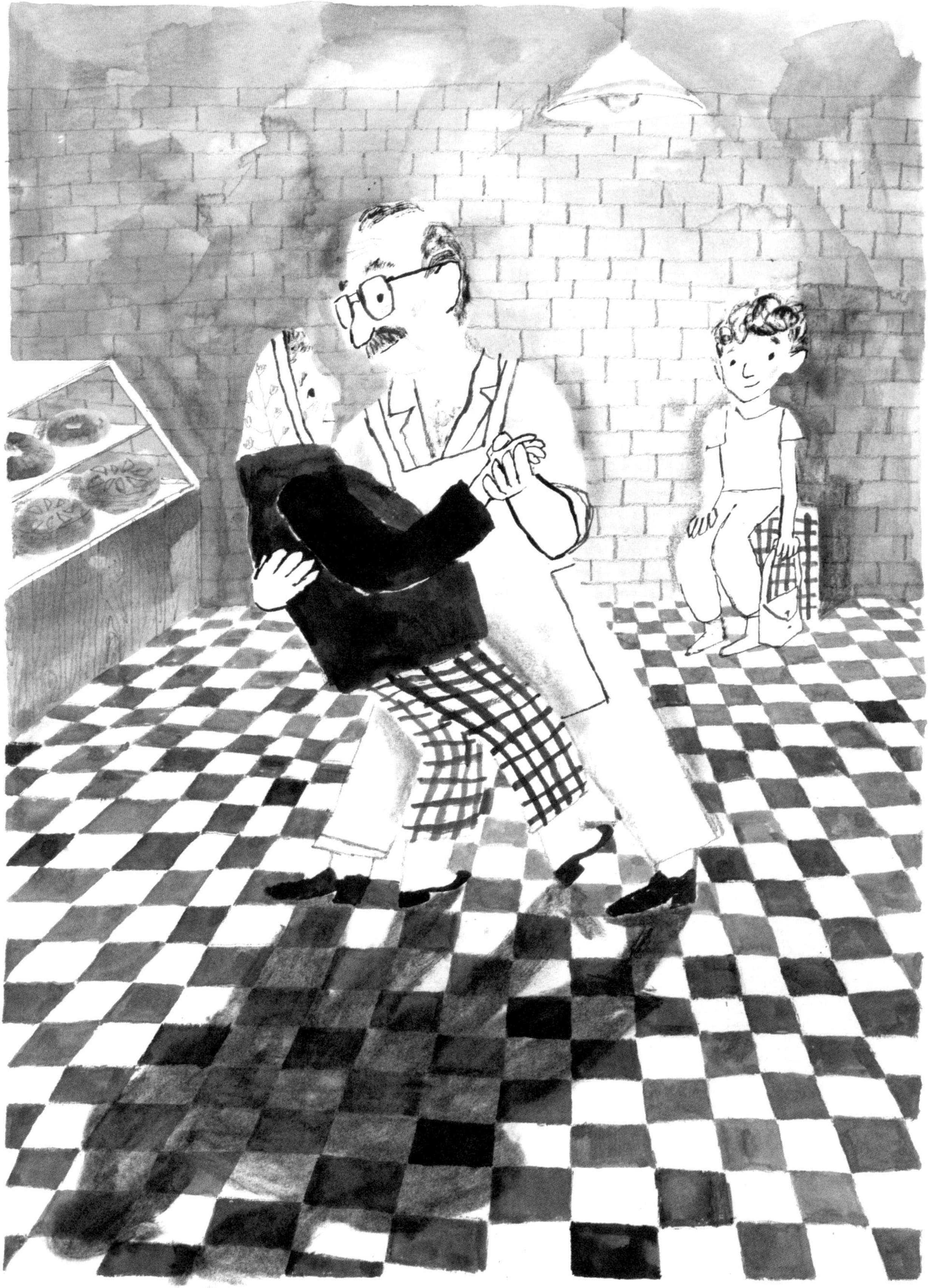

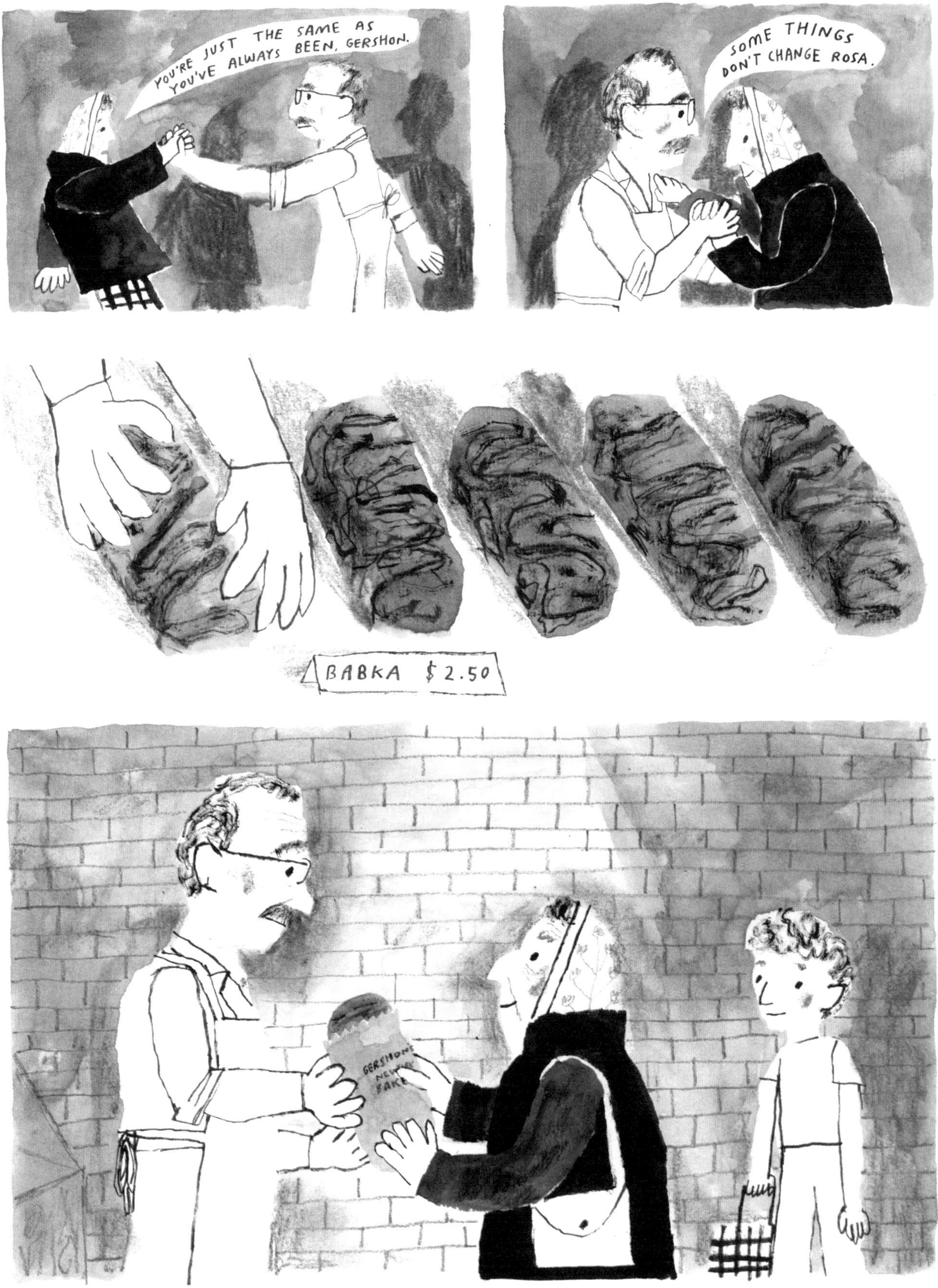
YOU'RE JUST THE SAME AS YOU'VE ALWAYS BEEN, GERSHON.
SOME THINGS DON'T CHANGE ROSA.
BABKA $2.50

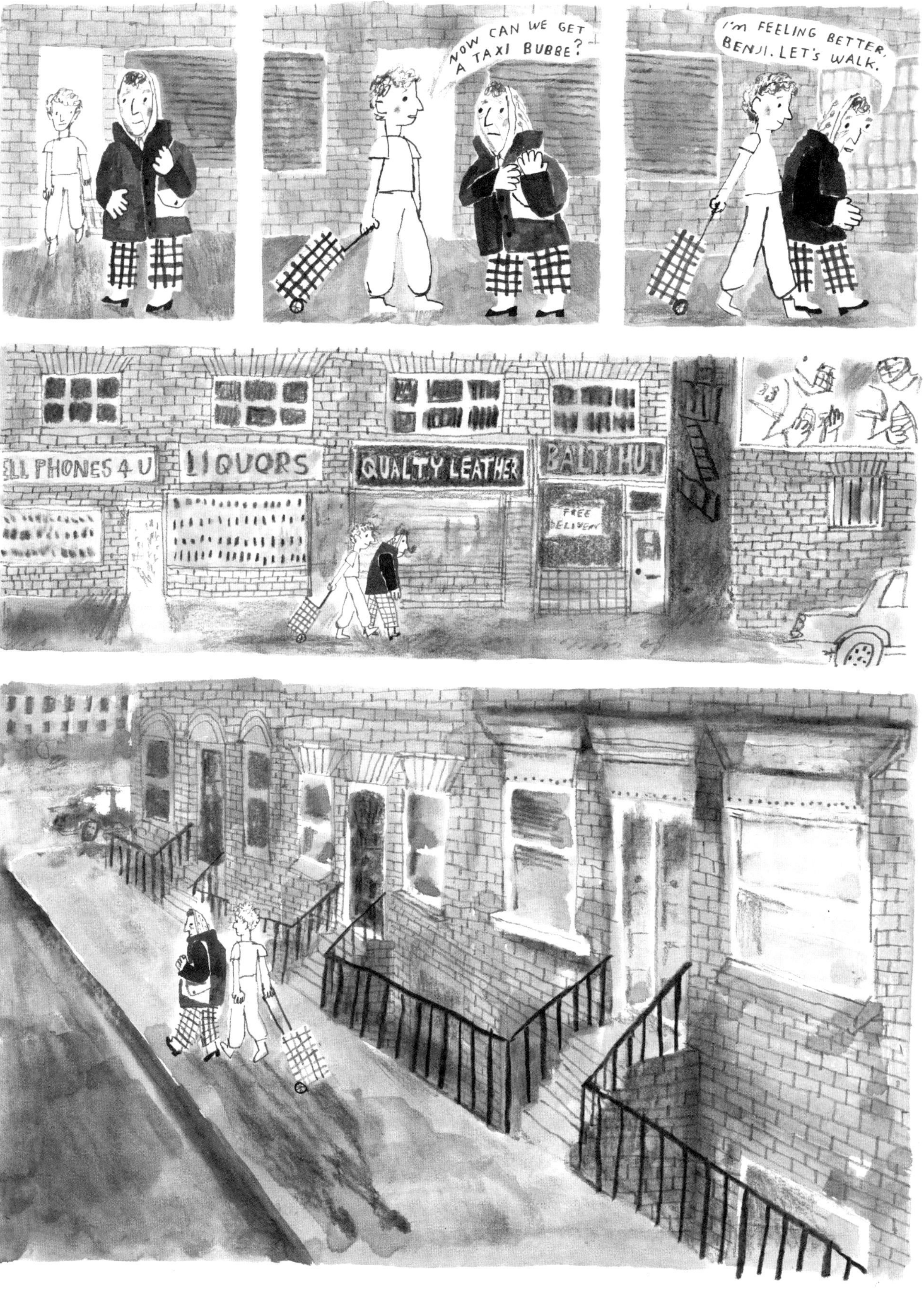
NOW CAN WE GET A TAXI BUBBE?
I'M FEELING BETTER, BENJI. LET'S WALK.
ELL PHONES 4 U
LIQUORS
QUALTY LEATHER
BALTI HUT
FREE DELIVERY

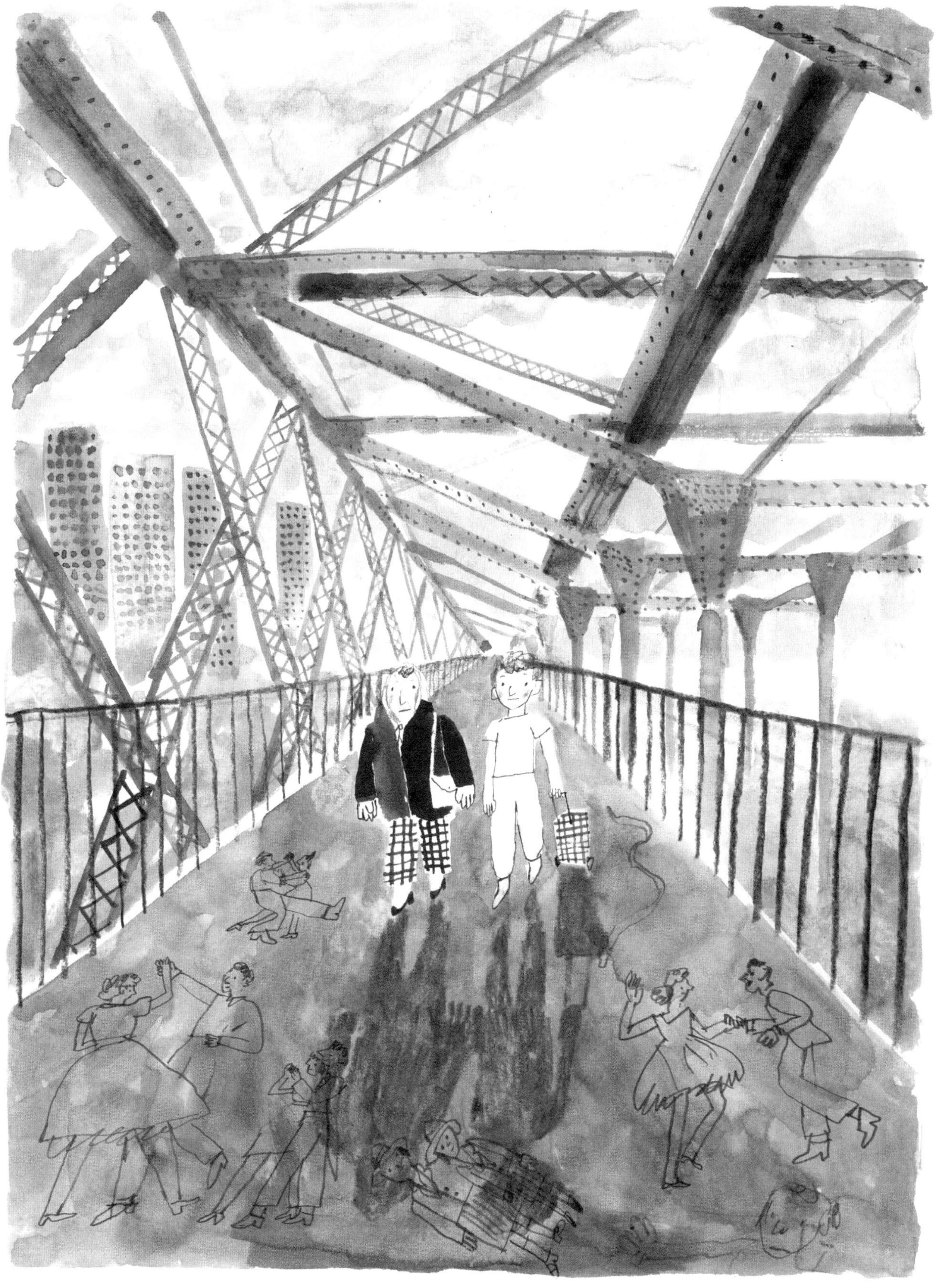

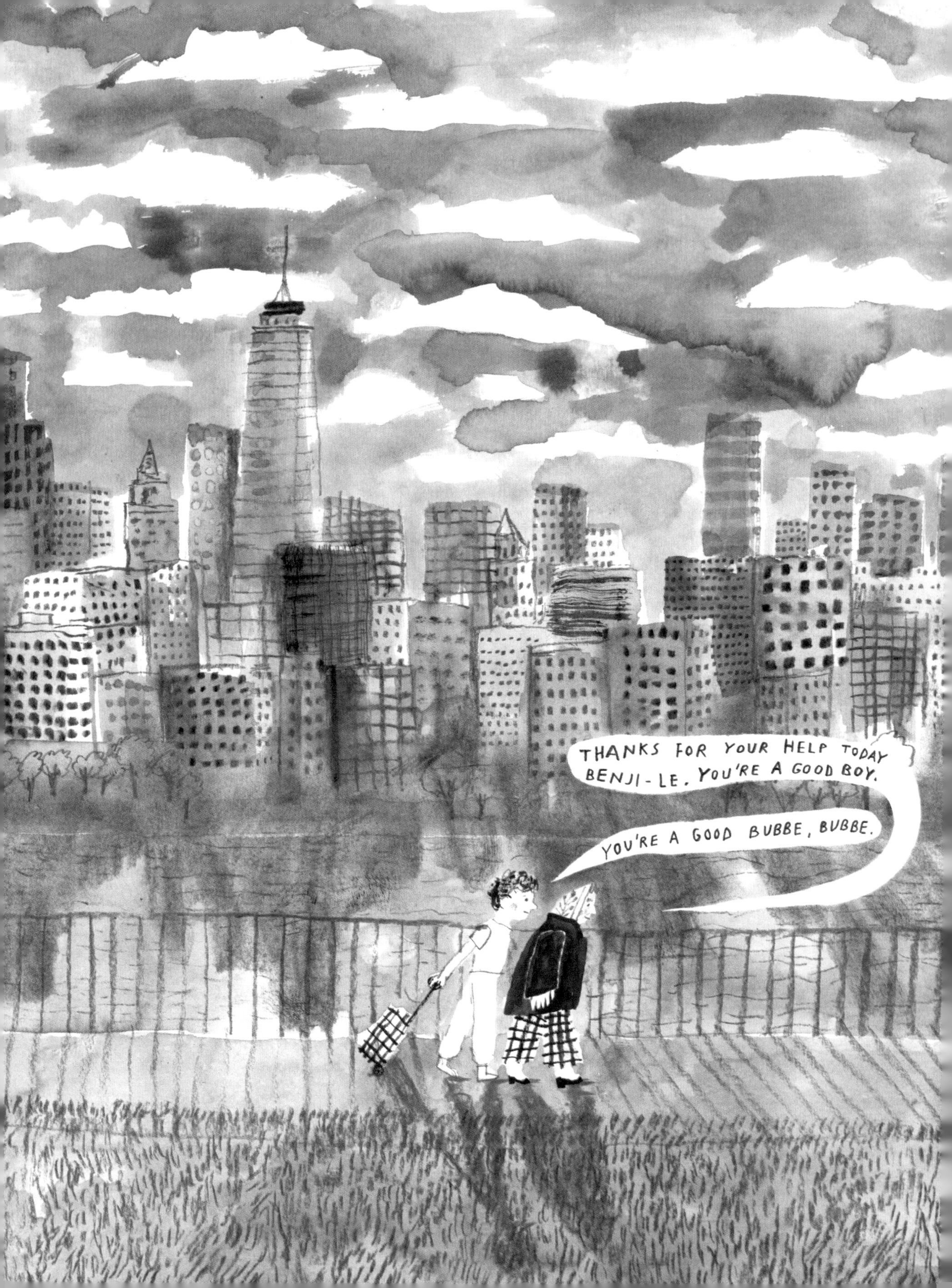
THANKS FOR YOUR HELP TODAY BENJI-LE. YOU'RE A GOOD BOY.
YOU'RE A GOOD BUBBE, BUBBE.

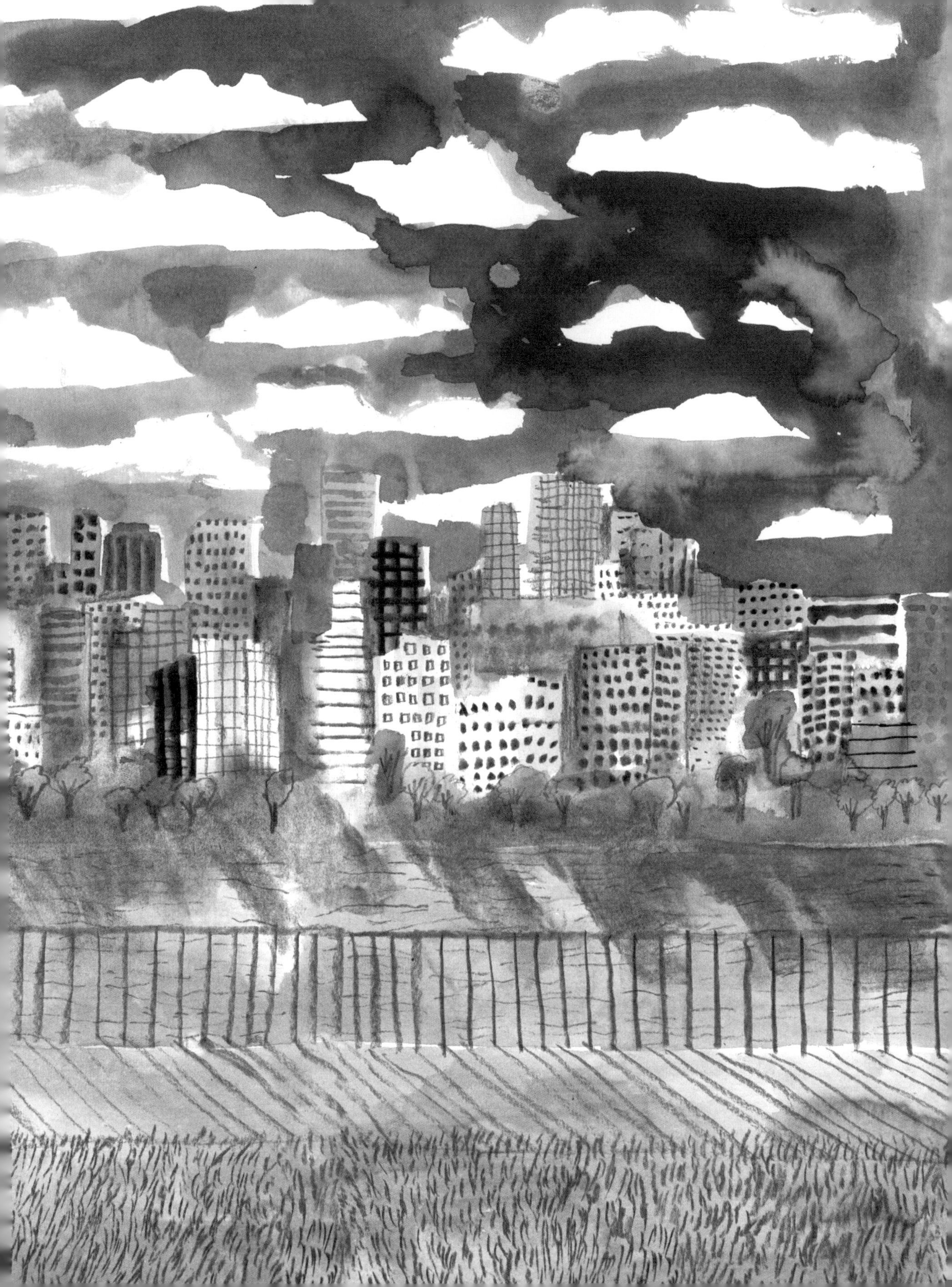

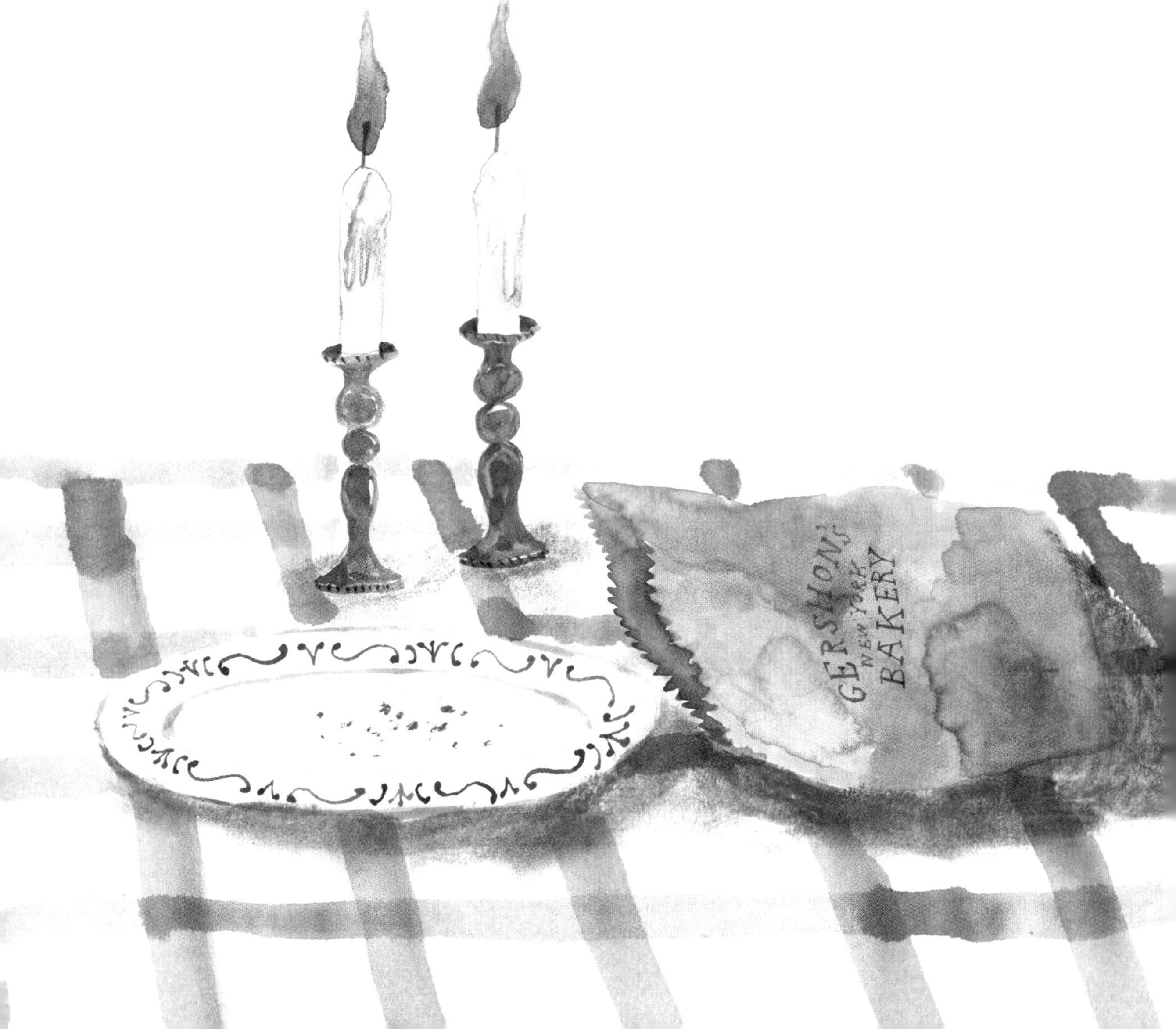
GERSHON'S
NEW YORK
BAKERY

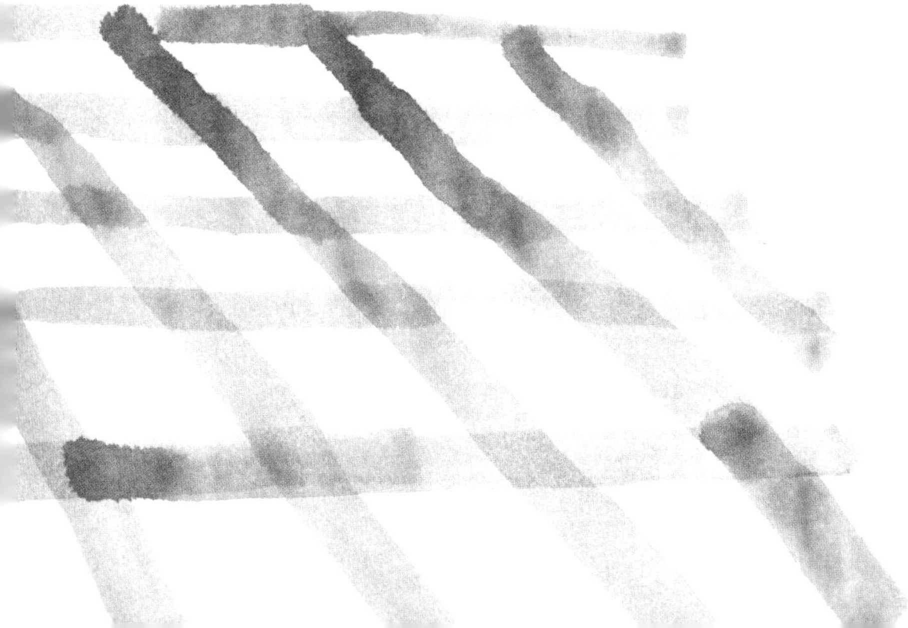

GLOSSARY

THESE ARE SOME OF THE YIDDISH TERMS USED IN THIS BOOK:

ALTEKAKER - OLD FART

ALTE ZACHEN - OLD THINGS

BABKA - A YEAST CAKE FILLED WITH CHOCOLATE OR CINNAMON.

BARUCH HASHEM - PRAISE GOD

BRISKET - AN INEXPENSIVE CUT OF BEEF.

BUBBE - GRANDMA

CHALLAH - A BRAIDED BREAD EATEN ON THE SABBATH AND OTHER HOLIDAYS.

FARMISHT - CONFUSED

FEH - YUCK

GANEF - THIEF

GEFILTE FISH - A DISH MADE OF GROUND POACHED FISH.

KUGEL - A SAVOURY PUDDING MADE OF EGG NOODLES OR POTATOES.

MISHEGAS - CRAZY

NU - WELL?

OY GEVALT! - OH GOSH!

SHABBAT SHALOM - GOOD SABBATH

SHTUSIK - SILLY

TSOIRES - SORROWS

ZAYDE - GRANDPA

ZICHRONO LE BRACHA -
BLESS HIS MEMORY.
SAID WHEN SPEAKING OF THE DEAD.

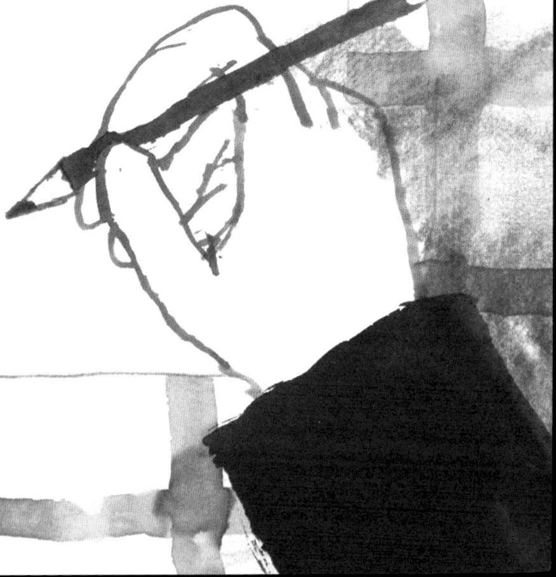

Alte Zachen

Text © Ziggy Hanaor
Illustration © Benjamin Phillips

British Library Cataloguing-in-Publication Data.

A CIP record for this book is available from the British Library
ISBN: 978-1-80066-022-9

First published in 2022

Cicada Books Ltd
48 Burghley Road
London, NW5 1UE
www.cicadabooks.co.uk

Printed in Poland

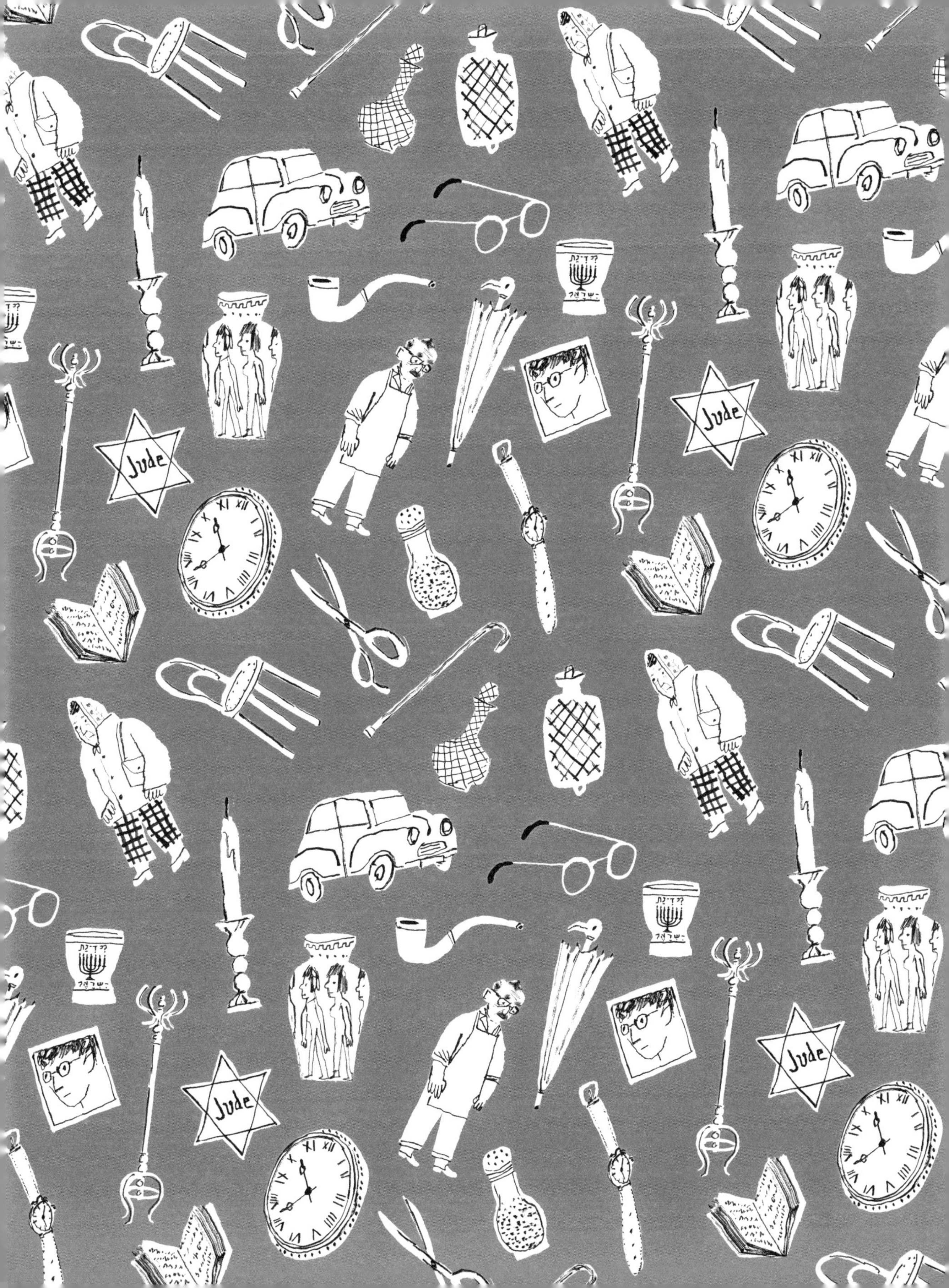
Jude
Jude
Jude
Jude

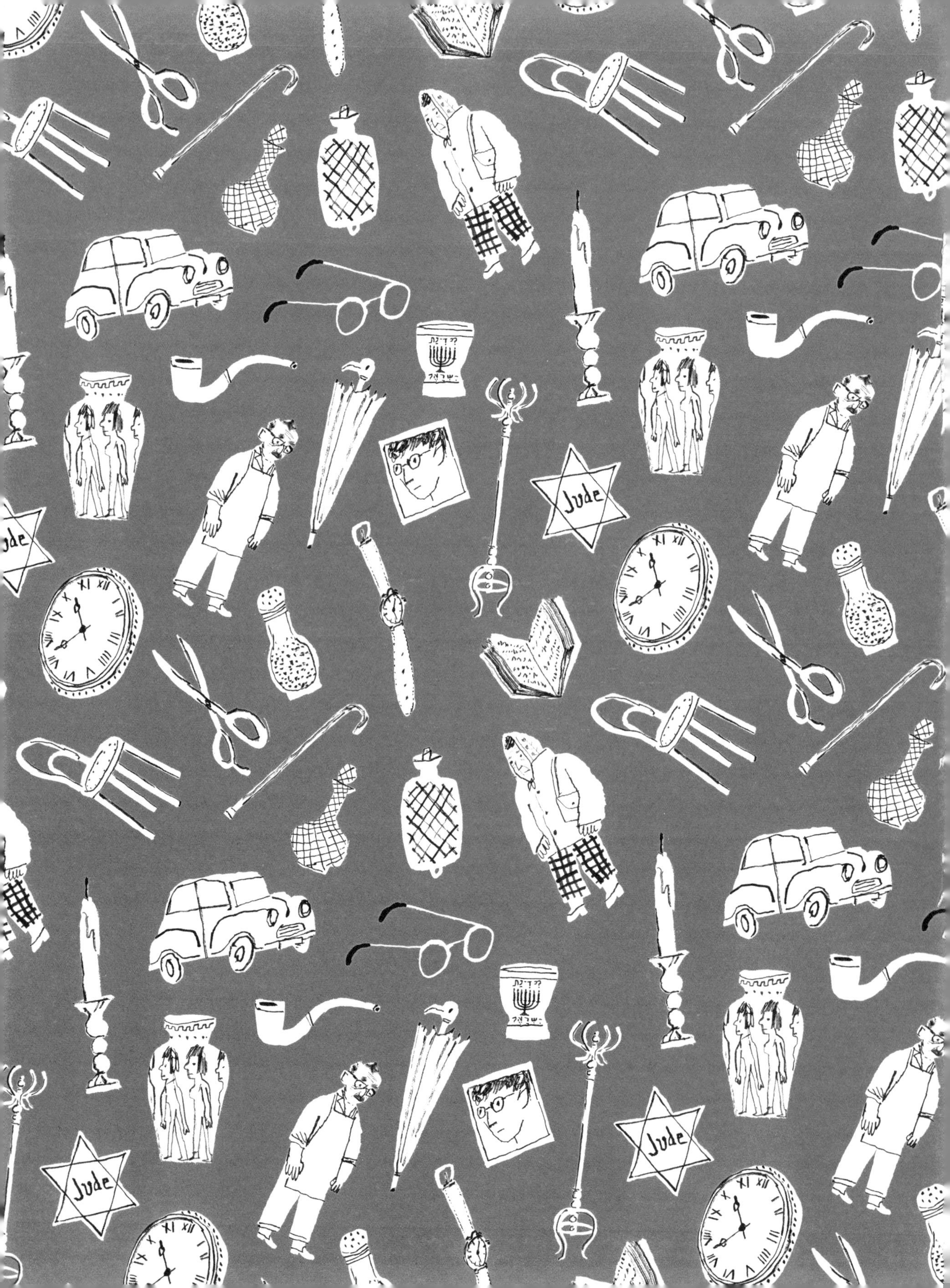
Jude